Reviews for "Sarge, What Now?"
Author: Bob Anderson

An Air Force Chief Master Sergeant once told me, "When I ask you where you're going, don't tell me where you've been." Well, that may be true to keep the conversation short, but knowing how you got to this point, helps keep you from making the same bad decisions. Sarge, What Now? is a lifetime's eclectic compilation of responsible choices the author has experienced and survived. While the dates and places change, military and civilian members will intimately identify with some of the very same situations. What better (and cheaper) way to hone your perspective and direction than learning what has worked for someone else? The military reader will readily identify with the real 'skinny' of military life and the civilian reader will find out what it really takes to serve this country. Ya gotta read this book!

—Gordon Bredlow, SMSgt, USAF (Ret)

Why should you read this book? If you are an NCO, it will give you insight on how to advance. If you are a commander, buy one for all of your NCOs … then sit down and read it yourself.

—Jerry M. Bullock, Colonel, USAF (Ret)

Bob Anderson has captured a vibrant and different atmosphere with Sarge, What Now? As a former Marine that served in combat during Viet Nam; he has told it how it is, how it was and how it should be. We need more books like this written about our military and their service.

—Carl Milligan, former Vietnam Marine Combat Engineer

Typical tale by Bob Anderson—truthful, insightful and spot on. Sarge, What Now? is his recent tales of true events, people and situations that can be taken as lessons for life.

—Frank Sullivan, General, USAF ANG (Ret)

Sarge, What Now?

Other Books by Bob Anderson

Anderson's Rules
Grandfather Speaks

Tac Leader Series
What Honor Requires
Night Hawks
Retribution

By
Jerry Ahern & Sharon Ahern
and
Bob Anderson

The Survivalist Series
The Inheritors of Earth
Earth Shine

Sarge, What Now?

Bob Anderson, CMSgt, USAFR (Ret)

SPEAKING VOLUMES, LLC
NAPLES, FLORIDA
2013

Sarge, What Now?

Edited by: Pamela Anderson and Paul Gregg

ISBN 978-1-61232-937-6

"The care and cleaning of lieutenants is NCO business."
—General Frederick J. Kroesen

This book is dedicated to the following people who impacted my career and my life. For those in the military, I use the ranks I knew them as at the time. There are many more unnamed individuals who impacted me and failing to list their names does not denigrate what they did for me. I can see faces but the names have drifted out of my mind. Some, I never met but still was touched by them. God bless them all.

To: SSgt Ivory Washington, Basic Military Training Team Chief, SSgt James T. Gray, Basic Military Training Team Member, Lackland AFB, TX, 1969.

To: Capt Edwin Schafferman, 21st Security Police Commander, 1970. TSgt Jack Blevins, 21st Security Police B Flight Commander 1970. SSgts Dale Harter, Lester Gentry; Jerry Olendorf, Grumpy; Auggie Zaragoza, D.U.H, O.C.; and all the guys at Elmendorf, AFB, AK, 1969-71.

To: Col R.W. Ousterhoyt, Commander 862nd Security Police Squadron; Ken Farris; Smitty; Tom Stoll and his sidekick; and the guys at Minot AFB, ND, 1971-72.

To: TSgt A.J. John O'Neill and SSgt Gary Jefferson 2nd Security Police Squadron Flight Commanders, SSgt Chuck Lewis, 2nd Security Police Investigation Section, Barksdale AFB, LA 1972-74.

To: The Clark Air Base Mini Cops. Col Sam Martin, 3rd Security Police Group Commander. Maj Tom Johnson, 3rd Law Enforcement Squadron Commander. TSgt Harold Bogard, 3rd LES D Flight Commander. SSgt John Moore, 3rd LES D Flight. Navy CPO Don Rhamey, AFRTS, Clark AB, Republic of the Philippines, 1974-76.

To: The Blytheville Mini Cops. Maj David A. Bond, Commander, 97th Security Police Squadron, Capt Al Smith, Lt Gregg Deane, SSgt James T. Perrett, SSgt Ron Phillips, SSgt George Champion, A1C Mike Stadelmaier, A1C Steve Engler, and all of the TNT Team. Harold Colley, Kathy and Randall Hall, Charlie Yarbrough, Vicki and Clay Jaco, Wendy Evans and A.K. Hendricks, Blytheville AFB, AR 1976-81.

To: Barksdale AFB. CMSgt (Ret) Jim "Dogman" Singleton, CMSgt (Ret), Larry Payne, CMSgt (Ret), Ike Watkins, CMSgt (Ret), Ray McClung, CMSgt (Ret), Paul Gregg, SMSgt (Ret), MSgt Mike Doelling, "Boss Hog," SSgt Dave Stewart, Major Buster Hendrickson, SMSgt Mark Johnson, Captain (now Major) Layne Wroblew-ski, Lt Col BJ Garner, First Sergeant (Ret) Jim Taliaferro, all of my Cops and all of my medical Troops from the 917th Bomb Wing.

To: Lt General Daniel James, former Adjutant General for my home state of Texas, former State Command Chief Harold Higgins and the other two Wing Command Chiefs, Bill Sivells and "Buck" Albright, with whom I served. I cannot forget former State Command Chief Sam Davis.

To: The men and women of the 147th Fighter Wing, Col Rodney Horn former Deputy Wing Commander and retired officers Col Bob Spermo, Col Steve Jones, and Col Lanny McNeely former 147th Fighter Wing Commanders, Lt Col David Blackburn; and finally Major General John Nichols, current Adjutant General for the Texas National Guard.

To: The United States Air Force, the Air Force Reserve, the Air National Guard, the Texas Air National Guard and the United States of America.

To: Brigadier General Frank Sullivan (Ret), Col Charles Beck, Lt Col Charles Carr (Ret), Captain (now Major Layne Wroblewski), then 2nd Lt (now Major) Joel Pittman and all of the troops of the 732nd Expeditionary Security Force Squadron and my medics, Balad Air Base, Iraq.

To: Ynnad Derf Nosugref—got along without you before I met you…

To: My Karate Students (Ski Li).

To: My mom Jinnie Ve Anderson and my brother Roger Anderson.

To: Carl Milligan, he was a Vietnam Veteran, a former Marine (there are no ex-Marines) and he was my friend. Semper Fidelis, Latin for "always faithful," became the Marine Corps motto in 1883. Carl Milligan lived that motto till the very end, now his duty done, the mission completed. Well done, faithful friend, "day is done, all is well, safely rest, God is nigh"; Semper Fi, Bro.

To: My son John Anderson and daughter Shelley Anderson-Moore and their families, particularly my grandkids (in order)—Sarah Jayne Anderson, Rachel Michelle Moore, Kayleigh Elizabeth Anderson, Joshua Robert Anderson Moore and Seth Matthew Beitel Moore.

To: Pam, my wife. Here you go, Baby.

To: Everyone whose face I can see but whose name escapes me; I salute you. They say that at my age the memory is the second thing to go, can't remember what the first was.

Together you all helped me become who I am today. Thank you.

"Far better it is to dare mighty things, to win glorious triumphs, even though checkered by failure, than to take rank with those poor spirits who neither enjoy much nor suffer much, because they live in the gray twilight that knows not victory nor defeat."

—Theodore Roosevelt, 1858-1919

"Lead, follow, or get out of the way. Take away all the reasons to fail, and you will be successful. Surround yourself with people that can do the things you cannot, but do the things yourself that YOU do best."

—Bill Babcock

Acknowledgments

TSgt Marvin "Buddy" Anderson, my Dad
Photo submitted by Jinnie Ve Anderson

In 1945 Marvin "Buddy" Anderson returned from Germany, met my mother Jinnie Ve Williams and asked her to marry him. When the picture above was taken, he was a Staff Sergeant. Shortly thereafter, he was promoted to Tech Sergeant for the third time.

For my father's efforts and heroism he was awarded the Silver Star. It arrived four years after his discharge; one year after my birth. It was about 18 years later that he told me he had destroyed a German machine gun nest, saving his troops.

Dad was not sent to the Pacific Theater to help end World War II. Instead he married my mom and raised two sons, me and my brother Roger.

"Buddy" Anderson was the first and best Sergeant I ever knew!

PRO ARIS ET PRO FOCIS
(For our Country and our Families)

Dad was a member of Company L, 3rd Battalion, 71st regiment, 44th Infantry Division, 7th Army. His name was Marvin Anderson but everyone called him Buddy. In fact I was a teenager before I learned Buddy was not his legal name.

Dad was the only son in a family of four sisters, presided over by his mother Alma. We all called her Mom. His father, John Tillman Anderson died when dad was ten years old. He became not only the "big brother" to Hazel, Polly and Maxine (twins) and the baby Patsy Jo, but a surrogate father figure to them. Dad was drafted into the Army and was sent to Europe.

During his time in the Army he was promoted to Technical Sergeant (he actually made the rank a few times. He was busted once for gambling in the barracks and once for decking a Lieutenant who gave a stupid order and was going to get everyone killed). He had his feet frozen, but was never wounded by enemy fire.

The men of my family had gone to war. Uncle Don Welch, Army Air Corps—New Caledonia, Uncle Delmer Gaby—tank driver, Uncle Buddy Cline—Infantry. These guys were my heroes, but the only time I ever heard any of them talk about the war was when we went to Caddo Lake and camped out or stayed on our house boat. Dad and Uncle Buddy drank Budweiser, Don drank Schlitz and Gaby drank theirs.

TSgt Milton Cline, my Uncle Buddy
Photo submitted by Debbie Cornor

SSgt Delmer Gaby, my Uncle Gabe
Photo submitted by Ann Campbell

Several times I sat while these men drank enough to let the demons out. After about a case of beer each, they would talk about the war, occasionally answer my questions and relate (always with laughter) the most terrible times of their lives.

The times when they were absolutely helpless to control their destiny, they could only follow orders. These were times when they and men like them fought all over this world for freedom. Good men and bad men died, not so much for what they believed in—those are ideals stateside soldiers expounded on.

They and men like them fought for each other, for their buddies, for the guy in the foxhole with them. They fought because they had too. They won. They came home. They took off their uniforms (most of them).

They took care of their families and raised their kids. They made a great country. Some made great mistakes. They became doctors, lawyers, teachers and drunks.

They ran businesses, sometimes into the ground, but they built the most powerful country on the face of the earth. They had pride.

Sometimes, when the right music plays or the flag is waving, you can still see those former soldiers draw their selves up straighter. You'll see a quicker step in their pace. You'll see the soldier they were, because that is what they still are.

This book is dedicated to all of our servicemen and women, in every branch, from every war. God bless you all! May God hold you in a special place, I do.

*****

Short Comments on the 44th Infantry Division and the 71st Regimen

The following information was obtained from a website about the 44th Infantry Division. My sincere appreciation goes to Matt Jolman at www.flumecreek.com and Clarence G. Anspake, Jr., President, 71st Regiment Veterans for their permission to use this information. God bless you guys and thanks for what you did.

*****

The Division was awarded three Presidential Unit Citations for battles at Schalbach, Fruedenberg Farm and Rimling. They successfully anchored the North end of the American line during the Nordwind attack of 1–7 January 1945. They fought battles at: Schalbach, Luneville; Sarreborg; Saverne; Furback; Drulingen; Sarreguemines (NORDWIND); Heidelberg; Mannheim; Darmstadt; Goppingen; Kempten; Landeck, Fern Pass and Fussen.

They captured the key German V2 rocket scientist team led by (Werner) von Braun, which formed the basis of the U.S. post war rocket programs, including the exploration of the moon.

They encountered 38 enemy divisions, 36 battle groups, 23 tank units, 21 home guard units (Volkstrum), 63 replacement units, 62 anti-aircraft units, 73 other units including: Hitler Jugend-Russian Volunteer Brigade-Hard of Hearing Stomach Trouble-Werewolf Commandos, engaged and defeated elite German units including: 17th SS and Panzer Lehr.

They captured the highest ranking Waffen SS Officer of the war, Commander of the Waffen SS 17th Panzer-Grenadier Division *"Götz von Berlichingen"* SS-Standartenführer Hans Lingner.

Sgt MacGillivary, a sergeant in I company, was awarded the Congressional Medal of Honor for personally crawling toward and eliminating several machine gun positions that were pinning down his company. In the process of doing this he lost his arm to enemy fire, yet still continued his mission.

They captured the cities of Mannheim, Ulm, Heidelberg, (and) Darmstadt; (performed) first wintertime crossing of the Vosges Mountains; liberated Stalag 1X-B. They captured Fortress Simserhoff part of the strongest of all Maginot forts, the Ensemble de Bitche, a critical position in the German Siegfried Line.

They were the first Americans to arrive at and to cross the Rhine in WW2, Strausbourg, (Strasbourg) Nov. 23, 1944.

Conservative estimates suggest the 44th killed over 20,000 German troops, completely destroyed the German 553rd Infantry Division and the infantry of the 17th Waffen SS Division, German 19th and 36th Infantry Divisions were rendered useless and accepted the surrender of the entire German 19th Army.

They had 230 days in combat, a record 144 continuous days of combat and suffered 6,111 battle related and 7,637 non-battle related causalities.

In World War II, the 71st Regiment, consisting of three battalions, was part of the 44th Infantry Division, which assembled at Fort Lewis, Washington. Headquarters Company of the 1st Battalion was detached to take part in the retaking of Attu Island in the Aleutian campaign.

The 71st was thus the only New York regiment to have units fighting in the Pacific and European theaters at the same time. This was before Dad was a part of it.

The regiment departed from Boston on 5 September 1944 and landed in Cherbourg, France on the 15 of the same month. This was when Dad entered the war.

Because of Col Paul Tibbetts and the crew of the Enola Gay and Major Charles Sweeney and the crew of Bockscar, two B 29 Superfortress bombers had decimated Hiroshima and Nagasaki Japan with two atomic bombs. I had the privilege of meeting General (Ret) Tibbetts in 2002 and thanked him for carrying out his mission successfully.

Introduction

I began this book on May 28, 1969. Of course, I didn't realize I was developing or writing a book; I was just living the adventure of a new Air Force member. I wished I had taken better notes along the way, but here it goes...

This is not just my story but it is slanted by my opinion. "Opinions are like noses, everyone has one and they all smell." All of the people I will introduce you to are real. The good ones you will meet by name. The not-so-good ones will have their names changed, and I'll let you know when that happens.

Some of what I will share with you are stories from others, comments by others, jokes from others and opinions from others.

My service spanned Vietnam (though I was never there), part of the Cold War, racial turmoil in the military, a peacetime military and attacks on our military and country.

This is not a tell-all or a how-to book. I tell stories, I'm a storyteller. Here's the first, I served 10 years, six months and sixteen days on active duty with the Air Force. I was out for five years before joining the Air Force Reserve. I retired with 32 years, four months and twenty days of service.

During these times, I saw our military struggle, watched our country go through "trying to find itself" and I was swept along for the ride. I've seen our country attacked and rally but I've seen too many folks forget what it was like in those first days and weeks after September 11, 2001.

"Sarge" is an abbreviation for the military rank of Sergeant. It denotes what is referred to as Non-Commissioned Officers (NCOs) and they are enlisted in the military.

A commissioned officer derives his or her authority from the President, the commander-in-chief of the nation's armed forces. Commissions are legal instruments by which the President appoints and exercises direct control over qualified people to act as his/her legal agent and help him/her carry out his/her duties. The NCO derives his/her authority from the commissioned officers appointed over him/her.

In the U.S. military there are several specific groups of people. Service members on their first enlistment are called first termers. Today, America has an all-volunteer military. First Termers volunteer or they are recruited into the military for a specific tour of duty. This tour will last from two to six years depending on the branch of service.

At the end of their first enlistment many decide that they have done their duty; or for a variety of reasons, the military is simply not what they want to do with the rest of their life; so their enlistment expires and they return to civilian status.

Many find there is a degree of discipline, organization, structure and excitement that is unlike anything they could experience in civilian life, so they re-enlist for more years of service. In today's military it is this second group that has the greatest opportunity to become NCOs. NCO status is conferred upon reaching the rank of E-5.

The final break-over point for most second or third termers is considered to be the ten year mark. Ten years of active duty service is halfway to a retirement.

However, sometimes the weight of family responsibilities, family conditions or desires will cause someone half way to retirement to "pull the plug" and get off of active duty.

I did it at ten years and six months. I was a civilian for five years before I decided to re-enter the military in 1984. I was able to retain my Staff Sergeant rank (E-5) and my goals were to make my "other ten" and make Tech Sergeant (E-6), like my dad.

By the time I had ten more years, I was a Master Sergeant (E-7) and a First Sergeant and I was having a blast. I was able to affect people's lives in a positive way. I was able to use my experiences to keep them from making some of the same mistakes I had made.

On the day I received my notice of twenty years of service, I decided I would stay as long as I was having fun or as long as I could make a difference. There were times I was not having fun and times I did not feel I was making much difference. Luckily I never experienced both at the same time.

So, why write this book? In all honesty, this was initially my wife's idea. She said, "Now you can say all of the things you've ever wanted to say about the duties and responsibilities of NCOs and the proper relationship between officers and NCOs." I liked the challenge of that.

Most folks have a mental picture of a Sergeant. That image is often one put there by the movies. Maybe it is John Wayne as Sergeant John Striker from *"The*

Sands of Iwo Jima." Maybe it is James Whitmore with his feet wrapped in blankets against the snow in *"Battleground."*

Maybe it is R. Lee Emrey, the Gunnery Sergeant from *"Full Metal Jacket"* and the TV show *"Mail Call"* (by the way, the R stands for Ronald). Or it could be Clint Eastwood from *"Heartbreak Ridge."*

Those of us that have served remember real people, Sergeants who guided us, prodded us, pushed us and demanded much from us. These folks were not from a "kinder and gentler" generation. They required us to be their replacements and to be the best we could be.

I have known and worked with a lot of NCOs. I was lucky to have good role models in my life. I had people show me what a good NCO was like and I had people show me what a bad NCO was like.

I've served with hundreds of men and women from the rank of E-5 (in the "old days" one became an NCO in the Air Force at the rank of E-4) all the way to E-9, the highest enlisted rank we have.

This book is to honor those men and women with whom I have served. This book is to explain some of the trials and tribulations they dealt with while performing their duties.

This book is also written to explain the duties and responsibilities of an NCO for the reader who has yet to attain the rank. It is also to remind those current NCOs what their job is SUPPOSED TO BE.

This book will honor those officers that understood the relationship between Officers and NCOs. This book is also to explain what that relationship is SUPPOSED TO BE and will explain that relationship to those officers and NCOs who do not understand it.

This book is also a way for me to convey some of the history of my branch of the service, my country and my flag. This book is a way for me to honor my brothers and sisters in other branches of the military.

Although we all "dog" the other branches of service, we cannot do without them. Those of us who have served have earned the right to pick on the other branches, but if you have not served—you have not earned that right.

Finally, this book is a way to leave something behind me for the "kids." The term "kids" is one I use affectionately about those folks I served with—officer and enlisted, young and old.

I believe that a good NCO is like a good parent. The skills are the same.

I believe that a good NCO takes care of his/her troops until they can take care of themselves.

I believe that a good NCO cares enough about his/her troops to discipline them when they need it.

I believe that a good NCO should put a "boot in their butt" when they need it and pat them on the back when they deserve it.

I believe a good NCO is a hard taskmaster that requires his/her troops to live up to his/her highest expectation of them. And when they make it to that level; he/she raises the bar higher.

I believe that a good NCO, like a good parent, tries to prepare his/her "kids" to be strong enough one day to leave and go out on their own.

Our first Commander in Chief, General George Washington once said, "The willingness with which our young people are likely to serve in any war, no matter how justified, shall be directly proportional as to how they perceive the veterans of earlier wars were treated and appreciated by their nation."

*****

Author's Note: Wherein I have known the author of material quoted in this book, I have named them. I sincerely apologize for quoted material where the author must remain anonymous due to this author's lack of memory or knowledge as to who wrote it.

Foreword

It is my honor to introduce you to Chief Master Sergeant (Ret) Robert M. "Bob" Anderson. The year Bob entered the Air Force (1969) I was serving as a major in Vietnam, assigned to the 7th Air Force Directorate of Security Police. In 1981 I retired as the Deputy Chief of Security Police for the Air Force. We formed the Air Force Security Police Association in 1986. I am the executive director and as such have been able to stay in touch with the developments in the career field.

Actually I met Chief Anderson after I was retired. In the capacity of representing the Association I am frequently asked to speak to the Air Force cops and thereby have been able to interact with the senior leadership. It was at such a function that I first met the Chief. He walked up to me after the program and gave me a copy of his novel. It was an interesting read and the beginning of a good friendship.

The Chief and I have one other thing in common—our wives have supported us in everything we have undertaken to do. You will be meeting Pam Anderson in the book.

The bottom line is I know Chief Master Sergeants. The U S Air Force is about as near to a meritocracy as exists institutionally. No one becomes an Air Force Chief who is not an outstanding performer. Some rise to the very top; no one exemplifies that better than Bob Anderson. What he says in *Sarge, What Now?* is important. It is well said and it is good for the armed services and a public that has forgotten where we came from.

What has Bob said that is so important? I recently collaborated on the definitive history of the Security Forces career field. We studied it from its beginning with the birth of the Air Force in 1947 to the present day. We traveled over 12,000 miles and conducted more than 115 oral history interviews, including interviews with all of the living past Chiefs of Security for the Air Force.

In one form or another, these interviews spoke to one of the Chief's main themes; i.e., success comes from learning all you can from the smartest person you can. How can you tell? Look for the NCOs with lots of stripes on their sleeve. When I speak to the graduating class at the Airman Apprentice course at the

Security Forces Academy, I tell the brand new one-striper or the young captain the same thing.

An important part of effective leadership is the ability of commissioned officers to work together with NCOs. To develop effective working relationships, both must know the similarities and differences in their respective roles, duties, and responsibilities.

Since officers and NCOs share the same goal—to accomplish their unit's mission—it is evident their responsibilities overlap and must be shared. It is not obligatory that the Master Sergeant, Senior Master Sergeant or Chief help train a young officer in his/her role. That is the by-product of the kind of working relationship that should apply regardless of the difference in rank. Foolish would be the general officer that ignored the advice of his NCOs.

There is a special relationship that can develop early in an officer's career. It is this relationship that the Chief describes in the book. The smart young officer will be looking for it. The top-notch NCO will be ready to share his experience and his knowledge to see the young officer flourish as a leader in his/her profession. This relationship must satisfy three elements of leadership:

1. It must be genuine. It cannot be a show or artificial.
2. The NCO must not talk down to the young officer or patronize him.
3. Know when to let go. If the relationship has been successful both will know when it is time to put the boss on his own.

Why should you read this book? If you are a Chief, you will be a better Chief if you take Bob's insights seriously and believe as we do that we have had enough management and it is time to build some real leaders again. If you are an NCO, it will give you insight on how to advance. If you are a commander, buy one for all of your NCOs ... then sit down and read it yourself.

You will meet a very special friend, Chief Master Sergeant of the Air Force Bob Gaylor. He's a brilliant man and a superb public speaker, and the example of what a leader should be.

In this book, which I believe will become a classic; the Chief gives us some of the history of the NCO and an understanding of what it means to be a Sergeant and what it means to become a Chief.

It has been my pleasure to write the foreword to this book.

In 2000 the Air Force Security Forces Association placed a statue at the Museum of the United States Air Force in Dayton, Ohio, honoring Air Police, Security Police and Security Forces all over the world. Just as we unveiled the memorial, a flight of F16s made a pass overhead. Everyone knows that it takes a special event with high-octane participation to get an over flight. Master Sergeant Mike Scott had been our man on the ground and I turned to him and asked, "Mike, how did you do that?"

With a smile Mike said simply, "Sir, Master Sergeants can do anything."

Over to you, Chief.

—Jerry M. Bullock
Colonel, USAF (Ret)

Table of Contents

PART ONE: MEMORIES

Chapter One:
Start of My Last Conflict

At about 21:30 hours on 6 September 2001, I said my farewells and left my friend Major Charles W. "Fred" Eaton and his wife Karla to enjoy the remainder of the evening's activities with his class. Formerly an Air Intelligence Officer, Fred had recently become a "professional" officer (versus line or regular officer).

He was graduating from the Medical Services Corps training school at Sheppard AFB, TX. The graduation dinner was a formal Mess Dress affair.

Fred and I had known each other over forty years. We served together in Alaska and at one time were both enlisted. He finished his degree and earned his commission. In 1984, he was partially responsible for talking me into returning to military service as a reservist.

Back at the room I poured myself a Jack and 7up and tried to watch television. Unfortunately, nothing on was worth watching so I decided to call it an early evening and go to sleep, but I couldn't sleep.

I was uncomfortable. I was too hot and my chest felt tight. I thought it was because I had smoked a couple of cigars that day and they had irritated my bronchia.

I became extremely nauseated and decided I must have food poisoning. I was sweating profusely and experiencing difficulty in catching my breath. I monitored my own signs for moving of the pain in my chest. It felt like a 50-pound weight was sitting on my sternum.

Had the pain moved, I would have recognized it immediately as a heart attack, but the pain did not move and I became more convinced that it was food poisoning. In 1995, I had a bout with food poisoning and had become dehydrated as a result. I woke up on the bathroom floor after having passed out. I was lying in a puddle of blood, which resulted from a broken nose caused by impacting the floor face first. I knew I should not drive and called for an ambulance.

Dr. David Willis, Major, USAF, was on duty in the Emergency Room when the ambulance carrying me arrived. The attendants wheeled me in and Willis approached the gurney.

"Hello, Doctor," I said. "I believe I'm having a bout of food poisoning."

Willis took one look and said, "No Chief, you're having a heart attack."

Over the next forty-five minutes I experienced a kaleidoscope of events. Dr. Willis began administering clot buster drugs and oxygen. For the life of me, I could not remember Fred's phone number.

Nor could I remember my friend Jim Singleton's phone numbers. The ER staff had called back to the Command Post at Ellington Field, TX; where I was serving as the Command Chief Master Sergeant in the Texas Air National Guard. They contacted the Vice Wing Commander, Col Steve Jones who notified Pam. One of the nurses brought me the phone and said, "It's your wife."

"Baby, I'm okay," were the first words I spoke. Pam was obviously upset and began to cry. "Okay, hold it," I said. "We don't have time for tears right now. I need you to listen to me. I want you to book a seat on the first plane from Houston to Wichita Falls in the morning."

"I do NOT want you to call Mom or the kids until we know what the verdict is going to be. I'm feeling better but still do not know what the next step will be."

I knew I had to get her thinking about something she could be doing instead of focusing on what she could not have any effect on.

"I need you to check our caller ID and get Fred's number off of it. Damned, but I can't remember it. Tell him to get his butt up here. He'll meet you at the plane tomorrow. After you have your flight information, call Karla and give it to her. I have to go now, I love you Baby." She was stronger.

About 30 minutes later Fred walked into the ER. "Well," he said with a pinched look on his face, "You look like shit."

"Thank you Sir for those warm words of comfort and encouragement," I said. We shook hands hard.

Dr. Willis came up at that moment and said, "Chief, I am not happy with the EKGs we're getting off of you. I am transferring you to the Cardiac Intensive Care Unit of the hospital downtown. They have called the Cardiologist on duty and he is en route."

"What are the options at this stage, Doctor?" I asked.

"I don't know but I would say that angioplasty or a by-pass would be in order. The Cardiologist will have to make that call when you get there," Willis said with a shrug.

In short order they had me in the ambulance and Fred was following. Thirty minutes later (it seemed longer) we were settled in the CICU. I asked Fred, "So, you know how to get back here?"

"Yeah, yeah sure," Fred said still with concern etched in his face and a distant look in his eyes.

"Fred, are you okay?" I asked at that moment more worried about Fred than myself.

"Yeah, yeah sure," Fred said and returned to the here and now. "I'm just going through my checklists."

I laughed. "Okay, go home and get some rest, I need you to take care of Pam tomorrow. Whatever is going to happen now, neither you nor I can do much about. One of us needs some sleep for tomorrow and it looks like it's gonna have to be you."

"All right," he said, not happy about not staying but knowing I was right.

"You're sure?"

"Get outta here," I said. Fred turned and I stuck out my hand. "Thanks Bro." Fred shook the outstretched hand and neither of us said anything for a moment. There was nothing to say and there was too much to ever put into words. "No problem. Keep your powder dry."

"Roger that," I said. "Take care of Pam. And Fred, if this goes south I want you to be the one to tell the kids, okay?"

"Done," he said over his shoulder as he walked out of the room. Neither of us had anything left to say.

"Thanks again," I said to Fred's broad back—one hand came up and gave a short wave, Fred never looked back. I would have given anything for him to stay, but there was no purpose to it and I would need him more tomorrow.

Man, I am freezing to death. I thought. *I have never been so damn cold in my life*. The Cardiologist, Dr. Cong arrived, he checked the EKGs and blood work and said, "Get him prepped, we need to do this now."

My chest still hurt. I was still trying to control my breathing. I was headed toward something I did not know nearly enough about. I had no idea what my chances were. I was utterly alone in a room full of strangers. Yes, I was scared— damn right I was scared. At that moment the gurney I was on slammed through the doors to the operating theatre.

My last conscious thought before the procedure began was short, succinct and eloquent, "Crap."

Inside the room was colder, even colder than I already was. As I was moved from the gurney to the table, it got even colder. Throughout the procedure there were only three people I would remember seeing—one male tech, one female tech and the doctor.

There was some kind of off-the-wall music playing. I realized it was to help the doctor to focus and relax but it was driving me crazy.

"Doctor," I said, "would it upset things very much if I ask you to find another station for the music? This head-banging stuff is going to make me crazy."

"No problem," the doctor smiled but it was obvious he was not happy about the change in mood music. "Now we shall begin, I want you to relax and I want you to listen to me, from time to time I will need your assistance during the procedure."

"Do you mean I will be awake during this?" I asked with incredulity.

"Yes, of course," Doctor Cong said.

"Look Doctor," I began searching for the right way to say this and not finding it. "I have a history with the martial arts and I don't want to react inappropriately. I suggest that you either knock me out or tie me down."

"I am afraid that will not be possible," Cong said. "Let us begin."

Crap, I thought. *Crap, crap, crap!* I focused on the empty room my Karate Sensei Joel David had trained me to find so long ago. An empty room, furnished with items my mind supplied. A room that Joel had said would always be with me. A room my mind could retreat to in times of stress and pain. This was a time for both.

The female tech prepped me by shaving the right side of my crotch and the juncture of my leg and lower stomach. I felt her swab the area with the betadine solution; I was still trying to focus my mind to "go away someplace else."

The female tech stepped away and Dr. Cong appeared at my right side. "There will be a sting now," He said to me and he was absolutely correct. The needle felt like a bumblebee sting. I thought, well at least he numbed the area. Three minutes later I realized if the shot had killed any of the pain I would have really suffered without it.

The insertion of the heart catheter needle felt like a one-way lug wrench being shoved into my artery, but I registered the pain with my mind not my body.

My muscles remained relaxed with no sign of tension. My mind was divided into two compartments. One compartment experienced the pain and the fear of the procedure.

The other compartment witnessed the pain and observed the fear but remained aloof from both. This was the compartment that would carry me through the procedure.

Because there was an overhead light fixture directly over my head, I could not watch the progress of the catheterization probe on the screen but I tracked it in my mind. My breathing was regular and my hands were coiled into semi-fists.

My thumbs protruded from between my first and middle fingers. The second digit of each first finger positioned on the thumbnail. My semi-fist would alternate between clinched and relaxed depending on how much control that compartment needed to exert.

After about twenty minutes, Dr. Cong told me to relax. After consulting the films of the procedure the Doctor came back and said, "We shall perform the angioplasty and place the stent." After another forty minutes, Dr. Cong declared, "very good, we are finished. There will be a sting now."

With those words he ripped that one-way lug wrench from my groin. Due to blood thinning agents, he put a pressure bandage over the wound and advised me that it was critical that I not move that leg for the next eight hours.

I was returned to the CCU where I finally was able to warm up and dozed in and out for the next several hours. Eventually, Pam, Karla and Fred showed up. The next three days were a mix of slow walks, bad TV and visits from my brother and son and their wives and my friend, Mike Stadelmaier.

Damn near dying is a somewhat humbling experience. Dying became something I decided to forego any time in the near future.

I was pretty happy that the Doctor said he was going to release me Monday afternoon. When the time finally came, Pam and I beat feet out of the hospital.

I have to say in all honesty that the folks there treated me wonderfully and Pam and I both appreciated their flexibility and humor.

We left the hospital and moved our stuff to the room Pam had booked for us across from the hospital, then went walking. I had to do something more than the

210 steps at a time that I had been doing since Friday afternoon. We probably did a mile that evening resting only to pick up some items from the pharmacy.

We were scheduled to fly back to Houston the next day, so we walked over to the hospital that morning for breakfast. When we returned to the room the news was on. The voice over was showing one of the twin towers of the World Trade Center where an airplane had only moments before crashed into it.

Smoke and fire was billowing out. At that instant another plane banked into view and smashed into the second tower.

The date was September 11, 2001.

Chapter Two:
Aftermath? No, Beginning

By the time we arrived at the Wichita Falls Airport, the third plane had slammed into the Pentagon. I told Pam to rent a car and I tried to make contact with my daughter in the D.C. area. Her husband worked at the Pentagon.

That proved to be an exercise in futility so I called my son, told him the route we were going to take to get back to Houston, Texas and asked him to make contact with his sister and call me.

Pam and I drove home that day from Wichita Falls. It was the strangest of days and I had no idea what to expect along the way. After we left Wichita Falls, we drove to Bowie Texas and stopped at a Wal-Mart.

I had Pam purchase some food, water, flashlights, batteries and two blankets. I went to the sporting goods section and bought a .30-.30 Marlin and five boxes of ammo. After I had loaded the rifle, I turned to Pam and said, "Now, we can head home."

We found out along the way that my daughter and her kids were okay and my son-in-law had survived the attack on the Pentagon.

We found out my son's sister-in-law had survived the World Trade Center collapse. She had been in Building Seven.

When we arrived home I checked our supplies, filled up water containers and ordered Pizza from Domino's! It was surreal as I sat on the couch and watched my country react, all the time knowing I was now medically disqualified. This was not acceptable. I called my unit's medical squadron to find out what my options were.

I had the heart attack on the 6th of September, got out of the hospital on the 10th of September, took a stress test on the 19th of September and with some pretty fancy footwork went to duty on the 20th of September—on limited duty.

On the 21st, Col Jones and I went to what used to be called Enron Field (the Astro's baseball stadium). We had been invited to throw opening game balls for a matchup between the Cubs and Astros—this was the first home game after September 11th. Every kid who ever played sand lot baseball needs to have that thrill once in their life.

During the opening ceremony, baseball fans in the stadium were yelling at the Colonel and me, "USA! USA! USA!"

During the seventh inning stretch we found out there were 26,471 people there. It was an incredible experience, especially for someone like me who was in uniform during the late sixties and seventies.

In fact it was not until our folks came home from Desert Storm that I saw any support for our vets, except from other vets. It was truly a night to remember and I want to thank Col Jones for the opportunity.

Chapter Three:
In the Beginning

I grew up on war movies and heroes. Before I enlisted in May 1969, I had served for two years in ROTC and had attained the rank of Cadet Captain.

Shortly after that, I married my first wife and found myself having difficulty balancing work, college and marriage.

I will not lie about it; I joined the Air Force because I was scared to death about humping a rice paddy in Vietnam. I figured the Air Force probably was a better match for me.

However, upon my arrival at Lackland Air Force Base, Gateway to the Air Force, one of my drill instructors, Sgt James T. Gray announced, "98 percent of you Gentlemen are going to Vietnam."

That was my introduction to the real military. I was the lowest form of life on the planet. I had few rights (none of which I was willing to try to enforce at the moment). I was sleeping with fifty strangers in an open–bay barracks.

I remember standing next to my wall locker and being able to see my face in the shined floor. I remember thinking, "How do they get that shine?" A couple days later I found out.

During the next several days, life as I knew it ceased to exist. We became Rainbows, so named because we came from different areas of the country and arrived with different colors (shirts and pants) and when together as a group before we got our uniforms, we looked like a rainbow.

About three days into the process we were issued fatigues and marched to the barber shop where the final humiliation occurred. They shaved our heads.

I have to admit it was a remarkable experience. There is a joke about the barber asking a recruit if he wanted him to save some of his hair and the kid says, "Yes."

So the barber buzzed right down the middle of the kid's head and handed it to him. That really happened to the guy in the chair next to me.

We were learning a new lingo, G.I. talk. Beds were bunks, food was chow and everybody in the flight was either numb-nuts or ass-holes.

We learned that the Latrine Queen was a job that meant heading up the crew that took care of cleaning the bathroom.

We learned that your head was really "a gourd." We were learning a new way of life. Up before dawn and exercise, then chow, then the day began. Nothing from our past was allowed except letters.

We did not watch TV, we could not read newspapers. We might have been on the moon, (in fact Neil Armstrong landed on the moon while we were at Lackland) or in the desert for all of the contact we had with the outside world.

They had brought my group in on a bus just before midnight. I was amazed at how big the base was. Years later when I returned, I learned it was less than one tenth the size I imagined.

At 0200 the morning of my ninth day in the Air Force, I woke up and went to the latrine. I had my first bowel movement at about 0210. I know exactly where the expression, "shit a brick" came from.

Oh, and that floor shine? Turtle wax. Turtle wax and a kid named Murray Shoemaker who rode on top of the buffer to increase friction and melt the wax.

We had a kid name Mark Youngbluth who got the nickname Zorro. He had one of those black sleepy masks that he wore every night.

There was a guy I remember named Smokey. He was black and a wonderful guy. He taught me many things that have made my life better over the years.

There was a guy named Vitotaus Virskus—we called him Vito and his family was from Lithuania. He was a remarkable guy and I have thought of him many times over the years. I hope he is well.

I remember John Gross, Dennis Ball and a lot of faces whose names time has robbed from me.

Jay Smith and some of the guys became cops with me. Some of that bunch died in North Dakota when a Huey came down as it was transporting them to a missile site.

But mostly I remember SSgt Ivory Washington and Sgt James T. Grey. Washington was black and Grey was white. I remember the last thing my father had said to me as I got on the plane to go to Lackland, "Don't volunteer for a damn thing."

For the first two weeks, they played good cop/bad cop on us. Grey was the bad guy and Washington was the good. I found out later they would switch each class.

For the first two weeks, I was scared to death of Grey. He walked like a bull dog and every command he gave sound exactly the same. "ALLLAWAY HARCH!"

By the end of the third week, we could understand him. I never figured out if we became telepathic or what—but we learned. WE LEARNED. By the time the 25th day arrived and my wife and her mother arrived, I was proud to be a troop. I was proud to be one of his troops.

They sent a runner to get me. When I arrived at the Orderly Room I did not see my wife and she did not recognize me. I went upstairs to shower and change out of the pickle suit. It was the first time I had the latrine to myself and as I went to the mirror to shave, I did not recognize myself.

The word finally came down that I was to become a Security Policeman. I was terrified and elated. It was one of those pivotal points in my life where nothing would ever be the same again. I was going to be a Cop.

We said our goodbyes and I walked a quarter mile to the Security Police Tech School (I believe I got $.26 in travel pay). I never saw Smokey, Vito, Gross, Shoemaker or Zorro again.

I had been Dorm Chief during basic and I made up my mind I was not going to do that again. I did not want the responsibility or the pressure. I just wanted to learn and have some fun.

However, after pulling KP (Kitchen Patrol) my one and only time, I marched in and volunteered for the job of Dorm Chief. I had to get everyone else up and I had to know where everyone else was and a lot more, but I never did dishes again.

We learned good stuff; we went to places like the House of Hurt. We practiced the arm bar, learned how to make apprehensions, how to use the baton, how to walk post, how to shoot and clean the M-16 and the Smith and Wesson K-38 Combat Masterpiece revolver. We learned how to be cops.

In those days Security Police was a single career field and it was all men. I was there when it split into Security and Law Enforcement. I was there when women came in.

I served active duty at Elmendorf AFB, AK; Minot AFB, ND; Barksdale AFB, LA; Clark AB, Republic of the Philippines and Blytheville AFB, AR.

I served with the Air Force Reserve at Barksdale AFB, LA. Then I transferred to the Air National Guard at Ellington Field outside of Houston, TX, moved back to the Reserve at Barksdale and finished with a six-month deployment to Balad Air Base, Iraq.

PART TWO: THE NCO

Chapter Four:
Being a Sergeant

History

The following is from the US Air Force website, www.AF.mil:

The NCO, as members of the profession of arms, all enlisted members are sworn to support and defend the Constitution of the United States and to obey the orders of all officers appointed over them. NCOs carry out orders of those appointed over them by virtue of the authority vested in their rank.

This is done by effectively employing personnel, material, equipment, and other resources under their control. They represent the Air Force NCO Corps to all whom they come in contact with. Personal integrity, loyalty, leadership, dedication, and devotion to duty must remain above reproach.

As an Air Force leader, manager, and supervisor, the NCO must uphold Air Force policies, traditions, and standards.

––––––––––––––––

My Thoughts on Sarge

It is difficult to describe what making sergeant meant to me. It was definitely a high point. In those days, at the rank of E-4 you could be a sergeant. I personally believe the Air Force made a mistake when they changed that.

My rational is this. In the days when it was reasonably possible for a person to make the rank of Sergeant it also meant they were required to ASSUME the duties and responsibilities of being a Sergeant. Often that would occur during the first enlistment. That shift, moving from a troop to a Sergeant gave them a new perspective.

It gave them desire, motivation and responsibilities that made most of them better. We were growing NCOs and leaders. That process has now been delayed.

Now, the assumption is you could expect to become an NCO on the second enlistment. On average it also means it could take five or six years, possibly more. That is time wasted! The two years I had as a Sergeant gave me the training and experience to be a better Staff Sergeant, it was invaluable.

I got better faster, because I had to. Now, we are delaying that process and adding almost an adolescence phase. Men become men and women become women by accepting challenge, making mistakes and learning from them. We have cuddled (unnecessarily) and protected great potential NCOs that didn't last for that second enlistment and the Air Force suffered for that "kinder and gentler" process.

"Sergeant"
By Bob Anderson

I am a Non-Commissioned Officer in the United States Military. I have accepted the responsibilities and authority of that position.

I will, to the best of my abilities and training, perform those duties and I will continue to strive to improve my abilities through training and the mentorship of my peers and superiors.

I have sworn to protect and defend the constitution of the United States from all enemies both foreign and domestic, and to abide by the orders of those appointed over me.

I am tasked with determining how to implement those orders. I must do that under the laws of my country, according to my military expertise, my code of ethics and my knowledge of the abilities and training of my troops.

Additionally, I accept the responsibility for the performance, morale and welfare of my troops; for I am theirs and they are mine.

I recognize that the MISSION must be accomplished—that is my duty. I accept that the MISSION may require extraordinary efforts from both my people and me.

These efforts may require heavy expenditures from us in professionalism, humanity, sweat, faith or even blood.

I accept with sacred trust that our sacrifices, should they become necessary, will not be spent without just cause and honor. Should those efforts require us to make that ultimate sacrifice, I shall lead my troops with honor, ethical strength and the conviction that what we do may save others from our fate.

My credo is simple; "FAILURE IS NOT AN OPTION!"

I will lead my people with reason, consistency and fairness with belief in my country and the leaders appointed over me. For my job is to help my people do—what may not be done; to accomplish—what OTHERS may consider cannot be accomplishable. In other words, to make what cannot happen—happen.

If I have done my job correctly and if God has favored us, I will lead them back from harm's way to the bosoms of their families and to the arms of a grateful nation.

If fortune does not choose to favor us and we do not come home; let someone say "They did their best."

I may be a Sergeant, a Staff, a Tech, a Master, a Senior or a Chief, but I shall never be simply an E-4, E-5, E-6, E-7, E-8 or E-9.

Whatever titles, accolades or fortune may lie on me, after Dad (or Mom), Husband (or Wife) is a title that shall hold a higher and more difficult significance.

My parents may call me Son (or Daughter), my children may call me Dad (or Mom) and my comrades may call me Friend.

All others may call me by my rank. Sarge!

If and when my country calls, if my people call, if my duty calls, let that call be simply, "Hey, Sarge. I need you," and I will come.

—**Sarge**

*****

"What a hard time young officers of the army would sometimes have but for the old sergeants! I have pitied from the bottom of my heart volunteer officers whom I have seen starting out, even in the midst of war, with perfectly raw regiments, and not even one old sergeant to teach them anything. No country ought to be so cruel to its soldiers as that." —Lt Gen John M. Schofield.

———————

The Air Force Enlisted Force Structure

According to the ***Air Force Enlisted Force Structure***[1], three tiers or levels are identified for enlisted members:

The Airman Tier is the first level in the Air Force. This tier consists of airman basic, airman, airman first class, and senior airman. It is the initial tier of the three-tier enlisted force structure. As a member progresses from airman basic to senior airman, he or she acquires the discipline, skills, and PME (Professional Military Education) necessary to become eligible for NCO status.

The NCO Tier is where technical sergeants and staff sergeants transition from workers and journeymen to craftsman and supervisory positions as they develop military leadership skills and obtain PME necessary to become eligible for NCO status.

Staff Sergeants must complete their 7-skill level through upgrade training to be promoted to TSgt. SSgt supervisory duties differ from those of the TSgt only in scope and span of control. SSgts strive for greater supervisory competence as they function in their technical capacity.

The average Air Force wide active duty time for promotion to the rank of Staff Sergeant is 6.9 years.

Technical Sergeants hold a 7-skill level and are qualified to perform highly complex technical duties in addition to providing supervision. They are responsible for the career development of all enlisted personnel under their supervision.

The official term of address is Technical Sergeant or Sergeant. The average Air Force wide active duty time for promotion to the rank of Technical Sergeant is 14 years.

The Senior NCO Tier is where the top three ranks of the enlisted force structure are Master Sergeant, Senior Master Sergeant, and Chief Master Sergeant. Within this tier, personnel transition from craftsmen and supervisors to leadership and managerial positions. SNCOs are assigned duties commensurate with their skill level and rank.

Their primary leadership duties are superintendent, supervisor, or manager of a flight, function, or activity. They should be used as a chief of a flight, section, or branch; as superintendent of a division or unit; first sergeant, or, in special circumstances, as a detachment chief or commandant.

It is very important to avoid over supervision created by establishing unnecessary supervisory or managerial levels. Proper use of SNCOs allows them to exercise leadership and manage resources under their control.

———————

"It is the job of the senior NCO to mold, guide, and educate the officer to the subtleties of Army life. [Do this right and there will be] fewer problems in the future. The NCO should show the officer how each job complements the other. He should be shown propriety and the unwritten laws of professional soldiers. These are things that aren't taught in any school—except the one in which the NCO lives." —Captain David M. Dacus

Informal Teaching of Officers

General John A. Wickham, thirtieth Chief of Staff, United States Army, has this to say about the "informal teaching" of officers by NCO's, in his "Collected Works" compiled in 1987:

I want to emphasize the informal teaching of officers that only you senior NCOs in your own fashion know how to do. Every officer can relate his favorite story about how his platoon sergeant started his rite of passage as a lieutenant....

When I was a new second lieutenant, I was assigned to the weapons platoon, 57 millimeter recoilless rifle and 60 millimeter mortars. I didn't know much about these weapons. I knew a mortar from a recoilless rifle, but that was it. However, I had a Sergeant Putnam-Sergeant First Class Putnam.... Putnam realized how 'green' I was. He did a couple of things for me that symbolize how NCOs can teach and how officers can learn.

He realized that "how I was received" by the platoon was going to be crucial. So—before I even met the platoon—he came to me that first night and said, "It would be useful for the lieutenant to know the roster of men, and here it is.

Tomorrow, when I introduce the platoon to the lieutenant, it would be useful if the lieutenant knew the names." So I picked up the roster and I memorized the names.

The next day, when he introduced me to the platoon, I called the names off by memory. The soldiers stood up so I could associate the names and faces, and they were impressed that I had made the effort to know them. They thought I knew enough to care, but in fact, Sergeant Putnam was teaching me to care.

The second thing Putnam realized was that I didn't know "my elbow from my ear" about the weapons. He said, "Would the lieutenant like to learn about the weapons in the platoon?"

"Yes, I would."

So he picked a place in the field—and why he picked that place, I didn't understand at first—he selected a muddy field that was right behind the latrine…. Why did he pick that place?

Because after supper everybody in the company, including soldiers in the platoon, went into that latrine. There, looking out over the screens, they saw me in the mud taking instruction from the experienced platoon sergeant, learning their weapons as well as they knew them.

Clever, Putnam—he was teaching, and fortunately, I was listening and learning. Sharing with your fellow soldiers your knowledge, experience, and standards of excellence is the greatest legacy you can leave with them. The same is true with the officers you teach. And we never get too old to learn a little more.

———————————

Chapter Five:
Being a First Sergeant

History

The **United States Air Force First Sergeant Academy**[1] has this to say about the history of the First Sergeant:

The First Sergeant has always held a highly visible, distinctive, and sometimes notorious position in the military unit. While there is little written history and many obscure gaps, we are able to follow some of the evolution of the First Sergeant.

Standing at the top of the noncommissioned hierarchy of rank, they were the Overseers of the company's enlisted personnel. To this end, they kept the Hauptman, or Company Commander, informed of everything that went on in the company; whether NCOs were performing their duties in a satisfactory manner, that training was properly accomplished, and finally, that at the end of a busy day, all soldiers were accounted for in their quarters. They were the only non-commissioned officers allowed to strike a soldier.

In setting up the American Army, General Washington relied heavily on the talents of General Baron Von Steuben. During this time, Von Steuben wrote what is referred to as the "Blue Book of Regulations." This "Blue Book" covered most of the organizational, administrative, and disciplinary details necessary to operate the Continental Army.

While Von Steuben outlined the duties of such NCOs as the Sergeant Major, Quartermaster Sergeant and other key NCO's, it was to the Company First Sergeant, the American equivalent of the Prussian Feldwebel, that he directed most of his attention.

This noncommissioned officer, chosen by the officers of the company, was the linchpin of the company and the discipline of the unit. The conduct of the troops, their exactness in obeying orders and the regularity of their manners, would "in large measure, depend upon the First Sergeant's vigilance."

The First Sergeant therefore must be "intimately acquainted with the character of every soldier in the company and should take great pains to impress upon their minds the indispensable necessity of the strictest obedience as the foundation of order and regularity."

Their tasks of maintaining the duty roster in an equitable manner, taking "the daily orders in a book and showing them to their officers, making the morning report to the captain of the state of the company in the form prescribed, and at the same time, acquainting them with anything material that may have happened in the company since the preceding report," all closely resembled the duties of the 17th century company sergeant.

The First Sergeant also kept a company descriptive book under the captain's supervision. These descriptive books listed the names, ages, heights, places of birth, and prior occupations of all enlisted in the company. The Army maintained the books until about the first decade of the 20th century when they were finally replaced by the "Morning Report."

Since the First Sergeant was responsible for the entire company, he was, in Von Steuben's words, "not to go on duty, unless with the whole company, but is to be in camp quarters to answer any call that may be made." On the march or on the battlefield, they were "Never to lead a platoon or section, but always to be a file-closer in the formation of the company, their duty being in the company like the adjutant's in the regiment."

For any First Sergeant who has received a telephone call at 0230 from the Security Police or marched at the rear of the Squadron Mass, there may be reason to believe that little has changed since Von Steuben. To a large extent that is true, but there have been some changes over the years.

It wasn't until the early 1830's period that any significant changes came about. NCOs were already distinguished by various colored epaulettes and other distinctive trappings, but now the First Sergeant was distinguished from fellow NCO's by a red sash around his waist.

Another development of that period was formal recognition, in the form of increased pay for the Company First Sergeant. A new pay scale enacted by Congress in 1833 established the rates as follows: Sergeant Major, Quartermaster Sergeant, and Chief Musician—$16.00 per month; First Sergeant of a Company—$15.00 per month; all other Sergeants—$12.00 per month; Corporal—$8.00 per month; musicians and private soldiers—$6.00 per month. Compare that to the First Sergeant's pay in 1944 of $185.00 per month and today's pay of just under 2,000.00 dollars.

The regulations for the uniform of the Army of the United States in 1847 authorized the wear of chevrons on the fatigue jacket for non-commissioned officers. It also authorized the lozenge (or French diamond) to designate the First Sergeant. Indications are that this was the first appearance of the diamonds as insignia devices.

As the years went by, little had changed in the life of First Sergeants. Perhaps the most significant and enduring aspect of the position is recognition of the importance of the First Sergeant.

The Business of Helping People

The following was written by Colonel Charles A. Romeyn, in *The Calvary Journal*, July 1925:

"After many years effort, we at last got our First Sergeants a big increase in pay. Yet, I believe we have not gone far enough. They are the most important enlisted person in the Army, give them the most pay and I almost feel like making all Second Lieutenants salute them. The ones I have worked with in the past and many others, I would gladly give the first salute. The First Sergeant is the Captain's Chief of Staff. A poor one will ruin a good troop no matter what kind of Captain they have. And many a poor Captain has had his reputation saved and his troop kept, or made good, by a fine First Sergeant. Am I right?"

——————————

According to military history, in 1947 when the Air Force became a separate service, the First Sergeant faced some changes too. The Air Force First Sergeant became a position rather than a rank and position. The AFSCs for First Sergeant began as 731X0s with ranks of E-6 or higher. In the late sixties, the AFSC changed to 10070 and 10090 and at the same time allowed new First Sergeants from any career field. April 1971 saw the deletion of Technical Sergeants (E-6) as First Sergeants except those who had been selected for E-7. Recently our AFSC changed to 8F000.

In September of 1954, Air Force Chief of Staff Nathan F. Twining approved the use of the diamond device sewn above the chevron as the Air Force First Sergeant insignia. As the evolution of the Air Force NCO took shape with the approval of two new top enlisted grades, so did the evolution of the First Sergeant.

Training for First Sergeants became emphasized and in 1967 Strategic Air Command established a First Sergeant School. CMSAF Richard Kisling conducted a workshop in 1972 and set forth standards for manning, qualifications and selection process for First Sergeants.

The workshop also focused on the need for training and Air Training Command was tasked to meet this need. A career development course was written, and was mandatory for all First Sergeants.

On 17 October 1973 the Air Force First Sergeant Course was opened at Keesler AFB, MS, with CMSgt James Blevins as the course director. The course was voluntary and CMSgt Willie M. Walker was the first graduate. It became mandatory for all First Sergeants in 1976. Attendees wore the diamond insignia to the school, even if not previously approved for wear.

Yes, many years have passed from the caning of disorderly soldiers by the Feldwebel, to the inspector and records keeper of Fredrick Von Steuben's "Blue Book," to the sash wearing, sword toting soldiers of the 1830s, all the way to today's First Sergeant who exercises general supervision over assigned enlisted personnel.

Yet, one theme remains clear. The First Sergeant is now, and always has been, in the business of helping people.

Top

First Sergeants are often referred to as "Shirt," or "First Shirt" or "Top" short for Top Sergeant. One theory is that the term shirt dates back to colonial times. When supplies would come in, the Top Sergeant would get the "First Shirt" before the rest of the troops did.

Another theory is that the troops would take their shirts off to do manual labor in the hot weather. The First Sergeant would leave his shirt on, as he was supervising, not doing any of the labor himself. When someone needed further instructions, they would have to talk to "The Shirt." I don't know which is true if either.

Nor does it really matter; the First Sergeant is "The Shirt." In 1992 I had the opportunity to become a "Shirt." I had no idea what a Shirt did, even though I had worked with several over the years.

Shirts were "next to God" in the pecking order of the military. They were magical creatures that everyone held in awe. I couldn't believe I had a shot at becoming one.

When the unit finally called me, the first words out of the guy's mouth were, "Hello Top"! I had made it!

I quickly learned that being a Shirt or Top was one of the most time-consuming and rewarding jobs I ever held. It was also one of the most difficult. Over the next six years I served as a First Sergeant to Security Force and Medical squadrons.

Prayer of a First Sergeant[2]
By SMSgt Sherry Wielgosiek

Lord, give me strength this day to deal with one more troubled Airman, one more stubborn NCO, one more uncooperative SNCO, one more family in crisis, one more DUI, one more suicide attempt, one more sleepless night, one more deployment, one more short notice TDY, one more futile meeting…
Give me the wisdom to deal with my people in a professional, courteous, caring manner, giving them my full attention, knowing I have a thousand other things needing my immediate attention.
Give me the knowledge to make the appropriate referral, the knowledge to know when I just can't help them anymore.
And Lord, let me not forget my family, loved ones, and friends as it is their love which sustains me, their sacrifices which allow me to do what I am called to do.
Help me to recognize the good in all people, and not focus on just the bad I see daily.
Keep me motivated, Lord, to follow in your Son's footsteps, and minister to my small congregation, their smiles and heartfelt words of thanks are all I need in payment for my labor.
And Lord, should my strength falter, I will always look to you and my fellow first sergeants for more.

—Amen

Military Branches

The following is from *The Officer/NCO Relationship*[3]:

All branches of the military describe the First Sergeant similarly: When you are talking about the First Sergeant you are talking about the life-blood of the service. There can be no substitute of this position nor any question of its importance. When First Sergeants are exceptional, their units are exceptional, regardless of any other single personality involved. Perhaps their rank insignia should be the keystone rather than the traditional one depicted here. It is the First Sergeant at whom almost all unit operations merge.

The First Sergeant holds formations, instructs Platoon Sergeants, advises the Commander, and assists in training of all enlisted members. The First Sergeant may swagger and appear, at times, somewhat of an exhibitionist, but he is not egotistical.

The First Sergeant is proud of the unit and, understandably, wants others to be aware of his unit's success. For the first time, the title of address for this grade is not Sergeant, but First Sergeant. There is a unique relationship of confidence and respect that exists between the First Sergeant and the Commander not found at another level within the Army.

In the German Army, the First Sergeant is referred to as the Father of the Company. He is the provider, the disciplinarian, the wise counselor, the tough and unbending foe, the confidant, the sounding board, everything that we need in a leader during our personal success or failure.

––––––––––––––

My True First Sergeant Story

One day I took two junior NCOs and an Airman over to the outside basketball court. They were screwing up like Hogan's Goat.

I was neither kinder nor gentler nor was I touchy feely! I told them what they were doing, what they were messing up and how to fix it. All three had great potential but no direction.

Today, I would probably face a court martial for what I did.

I used profanity, threatened physical violence and told them "If you don't get your head outta your butts, I'll destroy your careers."

Six years later, one of them was an officer flying B-52s. Another was an officer in a medical squadron. The other left the military all together. Like Meat Loaf said in one of his songs, "Two out of three ain't bad!"

In the old days, I could make a difference. Today, all I'd make is a Social Actions complaint...

The military used to be simple. The old time military First Sergeant was the epitome of that concept. His is a thankless job—not an officer, never one of the troops, responsible for everything and everyone. That kind of position tends to bring your universe into clarity that few people in peacetime ever attain.

> While on a training deployment the young Captain and the First Sergeant were in the field. As they hit the rack for the night, the following exchange took place.
> **Shirt:** "Sir, look up into the sky and tell me what you see?"
> **Sir:** "I see millions of stars."
> **Shirt:** "And what does that tell you, sir?"
> **Sir:** "From an astronomy perspective, it tells me that there are millions of galaxies and potentially billions of planets. Theologically, it tells me that God is great and that we are small and insignificant. Meteorologically, it tells me that we will have a beautiful day tomorrow.
> What does it tell you?"
> **Shirt:** "Well sir, it tells me that somebody stole our damn tent."[4]

My Last First Sergeant

The story below is by Jim Taliaferro, he was my last First Sergeant, a truly dedicated, sincere Sergeant who worked harder than anyone I know on the dictates and tenets of a First Sergeant. I believe that a good NCO is like a good parent. The skills are the same.

I've said this earlier, but I believe it's worth mentioning again. I believe that a good NCO takes care of his/her troops until they can take care of themselves. I believe that a good NCO cares enough about his/her troops to discipline them when they need it. I believe that a good NCO should put a "boot in their butt" when they need it and pat them on the back when they deserve it.

I believe that a good NCO is a hard task master that requires his/her troops to live up to his/her highest expectation of them. And when they make it to that level; he/she raises the bar higher. I believe that a good NCO, like a good parent, tries to prepare his/her "kids" to be strong enough one day to leave and go out on their own. These were "some" of the things First Sergeant Taliaferro lived by.

Yep, Worth Remembering

By James "Jim" Taliaferro, MSgt, USAFR (Ret)

Those who serve and have served in the military encounter people, who impact us positively or negatively, but nevertheless, leave a lasting impression upon our minds and souls, and even bless us with a bit of humor as we reflect upon those relationships.

Regardless of how we remember them, they are etched in our minds throughout our careers, to be resurrected when least expected.

The personnel chosen are only a few who have in some way affected, even shaped my military career and changed me as a person. However, I am truly indebted to those who remain unnamed for the impact on my life during my global travels with Uncle Sam. Some are positive, some negative, but all are valuable and worth sharing. Out of respect for their military service, I may choose to replace their names with a term which best initially describes them to me.

Other than my recruiter, whom I cannot remember, my first image of the United States Navy was an older guy, mid to late 40's, rugged and, to use a Navy term, "Old Salt." But to this 21 year old youngster, about to be drafted into the Army, this vet was my parent for the next 3 months. The term "Salty," would be a word which I would come to love, but more importantly respect.

For in the years following, it would be used frequently to describe those who have paid their dues, acquired a certain level of maturity and knowledge. The Chief, a short stature of a man, maybe 5' 6", sported a "beer belly," weathered skin from what I presumed was caused by years sailing the open seas working his craft on the deck of many a war vessel; but for 18 weeks, he ruled with a gruff voice of authority propelled by the breath of the latest drink he recently consumed.

From what I know now, he was an alcoholic and many a night on watch we would find him passed out behind his desk in the barracks. Before we knew enough about life and the problems associated with his unconsciousness, we just laughed and pressed on, giving him the blanket of security of peaceful rest he and his fellow sailors deserved.

Now you may wonder what, if anything did I learn from this experience with the Chief. He was, in his own way an icon, pillar, yes some say a dinosaur in a Navy uniform, but he presented a stern persona which could have suggested he was the First Mate on the Mayflower or helped Noah build the Ark. He instilled in me a sense of pride in the service I had chosen to represent and as I shook his hand on graduation I said, "I am proud to be in your Navy!"

Regardless of what flaws he may have had, for that moment in my career and my "world," he was "My Chief," and that in itself was paramount in my career. *Yep, worth remembering.*

Radioman First Class Johnson was an interesting fellow, a Sailor in every sense of the word. Rugged, outspoken, sense of humor and knowledgeable in his craft as a Radioman or "Sparky" as the Navy term suggested. RM1 Johnson was indeed the first real "Sailor" I encountered as I reported for my first tour of duty on board a fleet tug capable of sailing across any ocean with the lightning speed of 12 knots. Having come from technical school to learn the foundation of my trade as a Radioman, now it was my turn to learn what being a "Sailor/Swabby" would be all about.

As I and the other newbies/rookies heard from the time we reported aboard, "now you'll see what the real world is like." I am sure no matter what branch of service you participated in, you may have heard a similar phrase, usually with a humorous voice inflection, accompanied by a wink or jab to the ribs from someone with a few more years in "the business" than you.

RM1 Johnson was my first real exposure to the world of tattoos; I mean every kind in just about every place. He had tattoos on the knuckles of each finger, both legs and arms, and even on the lobes of his ears. Yep, before ear piercings were fashionable, he had stars on each earlobe. I quickly learned this was an acceptable part of the Navy dress code.

My years spent with Johnson were invaluable and although we had just a working relationship because of the difference in our rank, he was a "communicator," a true professional who could perform all aspects of the communication field flawlessly.

These skills which I had learned early in my career were not just a job, but an integral part of the support the daily mission of my wartime vessel and the US Navy. I learned the crafts of my trade but more importantly, the importance of those skills to the overall mission, the global mission.

It is during this time I became fully aware of my responsibilities as a "communicator" throughout the long voyage to Southeast Asia(Viet Nam) in support for our Army counterparts stationed inland; the tactical interruption of supply vessels known as "junks" or "sampans" used to transport munitions to the VC (Viet Cong).

This was just one of our many missions during our eight month deployment, and a variety of new skills learned in my tool chest on trust and survival; but back to Johnson. He, for the most part enhanced my attention to detail and consciences about job performance. Through his mentoring, he and my experiences took me to another level of personal and professional growth. *Yep, worth remembering.*

Now, I have come to the crossroads in my trip down memory lane where the personnel I acknowledged have done more for my professional and personal growth than any others. Perhaps it is because these individuals came along in the latter part of my life and my career, at a place where, I believe, I have and had reached a level of maturity to accept their contributions and counseling on my behalf.

The First Shirt, a Chief and a Commanding Officer

By James "Jim" Taliaferro, MSgt, USAFR (Ret)

The depth of these relationships is, to say the least, immeasurable; for they involve the special relationship between a First Shirt, a Chief and a Commanding Officer. Those familiar will immediately understand the relationship and its depth, and those who have not experienced it may never truly understand, but will appreciate the dynamics of trust which form the very foundation of the relationship.

As a First Sergeant in the United States Air Force, I have been privileged to serve many fine commanding officers, all who have impacted, shaped and forged me in some way to be the best military minded individual I could be.

However, let me be clear, that as a First Sergeant I am honored and privileged to have served each of these commanders, for in the Air Force hierarchy, the loyalty between a "CO, Chief and the Shirt" may be the most complex, yet rewarding of any relationship three individuals could share.

As I press through this portion of my recall, let me be clear and respectful to all my commanders and their support personnel. While all of them strived to take their commands to heightened levels of competency, some would never see the fruits of their labors.

That being said, I am reminded of not one, but two individuals, who both singularly and collectively, have affected the latter direction and ultimately the depth of my career. Allow me to introduce you to Captain, now Major Layne Wroblewski and Chief Robert "Bob" Anderson, now retired, a team which as I will elaborate on shortly, were like no other I have seen in my career.

Therefore, to adhere to military courtesy and introduce the senior ranking of the two, Captain, now Major, Layne Wroblewski, a slender guy, maybe 165 pounds of "combat readiness" and he was, let's say, "high speed and low drag," crisp in appearance, razor sharp in knowledge and exuding true professionalism in all aspects of military bearing.

As a commander, he stands out mainly because of the relationship we developed. His "right hand man," confidant and advisor, Chief Anderson, affectionately known to many as "Uncle Bob," was a fairly big guy, solid stature of a man, physically fit, bald by choice with a deep voice which resonated maturity, confidence and experience; yet when in the counseling mode, it could be somewhat soothing.

Both came from very different places in their Air Force career and with a significant difference in age and experience, this relationship would be "one of a kind"; one which I would have the privilege of both being a part of and watch as it developed. As you may have imagined, with Layne being the youngest followed by me then Chief, the personal dynamics and levels of experience would, from time to time prove to be, well let's say, passionate, which served our relationship well.

I would be so bold as to say we "played" off each other well, yielding to each other's opinions and experiences to achieve the most desirable results; but back to Layne.

From the time he took the reins of command, Layne hit the ground running focused on developing the cop squadron into the finest in the Air Force. The characteristic I noticed immediately with Layne was his "fire in the belly," a concept some would embrace, others would fail to understand. To fully appreciate the complexity of my new commander, I will share just a brief snapshot of Layne's personality which I would come to appreciate and admire.

Layne was an accountant by trade, a bean counter, figures guy, you know the type, really smart, meticulous about all things big and small, a "by the numbers" guy, but also a visionary. While I considered myself to focus on attention to detail, Layne brought a new twist to the equation and forever changed the atmosphere and circumstances within my "AOR (area of responsibility)" and within the squadron; yep, "Captain Tornado" had arrived!

After Layne's initial in-processing, a few months had passed as he immersed himself in his work, arriving early, staying late, getting acclimated with not only members of the squadron, but also the responsibilities of his command.

As a side note, when I say a couple of months had passed, as traditional reservists, drilling only once a month, the actual time spent with your troops is maybe 2-3 days which is not a lot of quality time together. However, it was clear from the beginning that he was not resting during the days between drills.

As months passed and during that "break-in" period, I was just one of his Senior NCO's watching his performance and focused on understanding the method to his madness; observing as he directed support personnel to retrieve necessary data as quickly as if he were planning an invasion. To Layne, knowledge was true power, the more "intel" he had, the better he functioned.

I learned this about him immediately by the awards he had received as an Airman and NCO prior to his commission. They reflected his desire and expectation for excellence, both from himself and others around him. After months in command, he approached me with an offer that would forever change my career; the offer of being the squadron's First Sergeant.

I admit, as a Senior NCO I made it a point to know, I mean really know the troops under my command; but not only their names but their hobbies, their immediate family members as well, their birthdays and anniversaries. Monitoring the health, welfare and morale of our personnel came naturally; but the decision of becoming a First Sergeant came with some reluctance, partly because I questioned my readiness for such a position of trust, but also this meant relinquishing my badge and beret, visible articles of a Security Forces member.

Faced with a decision of monumental proportion, I did what I preached to others to do in similar circumstances, I sought counsel from my Chief, Bob Anderson who gave me advice I still pass on to others today. Bob took me aside and said, "Jimmy, the beret and the badge are not who you are," which resonates with me still in so many other areas of my life.

Bob and Layne's confidence in me for this prestigious selection was humbling and one I have come to treasure, and as I understood the magnitude of the position, I found myself immersed in my duties and couldn't imagine doing anything else. So, there it was, the most meaningful move of my career and one I will always be indebted to each of these fellow Wingmen. Now the work began.

As I began to settle into my new position, it cannot be overstated that I would be required to go from cruising speed to passing gear just to keep up with Layne who was "Mach 2 with his hair on fire."

As the First Sergeant, I tried unsuccessfully to keep up with him and reached a point where I started doubting my value as his Shirt and questioning my abilities to support him as a Commander; for it seemed the more I ran to keep up, the farther behind I fell, and my worth as his Wingman was in the infant stages of crashing and burning.

But just as the Phoenix was resurrected out of the ashes, Layne mentored with me on his expectations of our relationship and for the first time, I got it. In this conversation he offered me a few choice words, which I am thankful I took to heart.

He said, "I will give you many things to do, sometimes as fast as I think of them, and depending on where I'm in at the moment, could give you the impression that the last task out of my mouth is the most important and you need to drop everything. Your job, unless I tell you otherwise, is to prioritize these tasks based on what you believe should be accomplished first to support my request and the squadron. If you don't, you'll burn yourself out."

So with all of the other duties thrust upon him, he tossed me the life ring and helped me define my role as a First Sergeant. In our short time together, we would have many, Commander/Shirt, Layne/Jim chats, conversations which would prove to be invaluable in our relationship both professionally and personally. It was in many of those mentoring moments for both of us, that disagreements met head on, but compromise and solutions were developed.

Those conversations allowed me the privilege of understanding and admiring the person behind the badge. Probably the most important aspect of this relationship was the relationship. The trust and respect which developed between Layne, Bob and I, our "Triad," was not only instrumental in setting the sail for the future of the squadron and its members, but fostered our personal respect for each other as well.

Many people in the workplace rarely have the latitude to engage in honest, often heated dialogue with their superiors or upper management, where personal opinions or differences in management or personal philosophy are aired without fear of retaliation. This type of relationship is, as the credit card commercial states, "Priceless."

The real beauty is the promise, the pact, the binding agreement if you will, between us that when behind closed doors all was out on the table; but when all was heard, the final decision was Layne's and as we all would exit his office, we were "one" voice, united in the decision, sharing the responsibility of the decision. This was real management and commitment.

Layne was all about business with his entire focus on managing the squadron and developing the best trained, combat ready personnel possible; a concept I admired and embraced, but would learn would be foreign to other members, including those entrusted to lead.

I remember one instance where Layne was very hesitant about allowing a troop to deploy into a combat zone because of the lack of the job skills Layne felt were required. Layne stated openly, that if something tragic happened to the member, he would have a difficult time justifying to the family why their loved one was allowed to deploy lacking the necessary skill sets for survival.

This was Layne's level of commitment, his core beliefs were attributes worth emulating.

Layne's effectiveness can be attributed in part by the counsel he received from Chief Robert "Uncle Bob" Anderson (Retired). Bob was/is a great mentor, philosopher and all around good guy who either liked you or he didn't. And usually there was no doubt where you stood—not much room for grey, just tolerance.

In my observations, Bob was about mission accomplishment, civilian or military, getting the most mileage using the resources available, which meant people as well. Regardless of where Bob was in his life, military, author or on the lecture circuit, he demanded of himself and others true professionalism, and I believe his mission or motto, was/is to affect change in people's lives, to help them grow to see their true possibilities.

If you listened and heard, he always had a valuable nugget to leave with you and it was your choice to embrace it or leave it on the table. In my trip down memory lane, one of the fondest and funniest memories of Bob revolved around one of his methods of personal counseling, for regardless of your rank, Bob's sessions had a bit of a twist.

Each opportunity for counseling, depending on seriousness of the issue at hand, instead of calling you into a traditional office for your "one on one," Bob wanted solitude and focus, not so much for him, but for you to hear and absorb what he had to impart upon you. So with just four little, but impactful words, "let's take a ride," you were taking a road trip in someone's vehicle and getting Bob's undivided attention with no means of escape.

Those of us who were privileged to get this personal attention, laugh about it still. Bob remains a great friend, confidant and mentor whom I feel comfortable calling at any time about anything; for I know Bob will tell it like it is, as he sees it, leaving it up to me to take it or leave it on the table. In retrospect, I confess, those times when I have chosen to leave it on the table, I usually regretted my choice, but as he would say, "it is, what it is, get over it."

Nothing makes a point like sharing an experience. One specific situation I remember where I was at a crossroads, contemplating giving up my diamond to integrate back into my cop career field with the plan on being the next Security Forces Manager, the Chief in Charge, a move Bob believed would be in the best interest of the squadron and my career. However, loving being a First Sergeant, I chose to stay the "Shirt" and seek promotion within the Diamond ranks, by seeking opportunity in other squadrons.

This decision would prove fruitless and I resolved myself to remain a Master Sergeant for the duration of my military career, and as Uncle Bob would say, "Top, this is all there is."

Yes, good times and memories, all beneficial to me in my growth as a person and a "Shirt." I am thankful for the mentoring received, the friendship developed with Layne and Bob—*Yep, worth remembering!*

Chapter Six:
Being a Chief

History

The following is from the US Air Force website, <u>www.AF.mil</u>:

Chief Master Sergeant (CMSgt) is the ninth, and highest, enlisted rank in the U.S. Air Force, just above Senior Master Sergeant, and is a senior non-commissioned officer. The official term of address is "Chief Master Sergeant" or "Chief."

Attaining the rank of Chief Master Sergeant is the pinnacle of an Air Force enlisted member's career. Some Chief Master Sergeants manage the efforts of all enlisted personnel within their unit or major subsection thereof, while others run major staff functions at higher headquarters levels.

All Chief Master Sergeants are expected to serve as mentors for company-grade and field-grade commissioned officers, as well as non-commissioned officers and junior enlisted members, and to serve as advisors to unit commanders and senior officers.

By federal law, only one percent of the Air Force enlisted force may hold the rank of Chief Master Sergeant.

When this rank was created by the Air Force in the 1950s, a decision was made to use the Native American Chief as the symbol of this rank. That decision was made to convey the highest form of honor.

———————————

Symbol

The choice was made to honor that symbol (the Native American Chief) in order to honor another symbol (the Chief Master Sergeant). I have included both the history of the rank and the Chief's Creed for your information and enjoyment.

I was particularly honored by this promotion because my paternal grandmother, Alma, "Mom" Anderson was French and Indian. Her maiden name was DeShazier and she was part Cherokee. I had always been intrigued by the fact that I was part Indian (the term Native American had not yet come into play when I was a child).

Crazy Horse, Sitting Bull, Red Cloud and Cochise were as much my heroes as Roy Rogers and the Long Ranger. When I became a Chief, it allowed me to exercise my heritage. I began researching my roots and found I was one of the "lost ones."

My family had never registered on any of the Indian Roles. You see in those days, being French and being Indian was not held in high esteem.

When I became a Chief, I began to identify with my heritage. It is more socially acceptable today. I obtained a feathered "war bonnet," something I had wanted since I was a child. I obtained some pipestone and carved a pipe. I had been making dream catchers for several years and continued.

Someone once said, "Old Truths are simple truths and they are just as relevant today as they were the first time they were spoken." It reaffirmed that technology has improved, but the people using the technology have not changed except as to how the technology has made them smarter.

Over the next several years, one of my first heartbreaks was learning how many E-9s there were and how few were Chiefs.

Although the Air Force had been an independent service since 1947, the rank of Chief Master Sergeant did not come into being until the authorization of the Military Pay Act of 1958 which established the pay grades of E-8 and E-9, but without specifying titles for those pay grades. It wasn't until late 1958 that the title of Chief Master Sergeant (and the accompanying rank insignia) was decided upon.

The original Chief Master Sergeant rank insignia (1958–1994) consisted of two chevrons on top, three stripes in the middle, and three rockers on bottom.

Until his retirement in 2003, Chief Master Sergeant Norman Marous was the Air Force's most senior Chief Master Sergeant, having served in the Air Force since 1962. Marous left active duty in 1962 to spend 22 years in the USAF Reserve and National Guard before returning to active duty as a Chief Master Sergeant in 1989.

Chiefs Creed[1]

Be it known to all who see these presents, that
Chief Master Sergeant _____
has been inducted into the membership of the Chief's
Group upon elevation to the grade of Chief Master Sergeant
in the United States Air Force. Implicit in individual
membership in this select group is the creed that its
members are individually to be regarded as people...
who cannot be bought;
whose word is their bond;
who put character above wealth;
who possess opinions and a will;
who are larger than their vocations;
who will not lose their individuality in a crowd;
who do not hesitate to take chances;
who will be as honest in small things as in great ones;
who will make no compromise with wrong;
whose ambitions are not confined to their own selfish
desires and interests;
who will not say they do it "because everybody else does it";
who are true to their friends through good report and evil
report, in adversity as well as prosperity;
who do not believe that shrewdness, cunning, and
hard-headedness are the best qualities for winning success;
who are not ashamed or afraid to stand for the truth when it is
unpopular, who can say "no" with emphasis, although all the
world is saying "yes."

Chief as Leader

Sadly, I must point out that the Chief's Creed has now been done away with by the Air Force. I personally think this was a mistake, but no one asked me.

In my opinion, this was a "politically correct" decision that's had dynamic and ongoing consequences. Consequences our officers never understood and the NCO Corps allowed.

When I was on TDY to another base, I was billeted in Chief's Quarters. These are nicer than average military billeting. It wasn't that I was better than the troops, it was a privilege based on the rank.

Many times, younger airmen would stop by to visit, complain or get career counseling. They generally were impressed with the room. I used those rooms as a motivation technique. It was a physical thing that they could see, it was a goal for them to attain.

See if everyone lives the same way, if there is no difference between the ranks except money; it is much harder to instill a desire for improvement.

Leaders MUST stand apart! Their job is different from the troops. Their job is to lead. Their job is to motivate. Many leaders, both officer and NCO forget this basic tenant.

They develop a "friendship" with the troops. Now this doesn't mean you can't be friendly but it is like the parent that says they are "best friends" with their kids.

The children have friends, but they only (prior to the destruction wrought on the family) have only one father or mother.

The job of that father or mother is different from the job of a friend. When that difference is allowed to degrade or be destroyed, you have eliminated the most important aspect of the father, the mother, the leader.

E-9 vs. Chief

I said earlier that over the years, one of my first heartbreaks was learning how many E-9s we had and how few were Chiefs. Mostly, I think they began to view themselves as "politicians" more concerned with "winning" than "doing."

A few changed when they put on that last rocker; they became more concerned with keeping the stripes rather than "being" the stripes. When you are more concerned with keeping them than being them, you don't deserve them.

When you begin to ignore (or now never hear) the Chief's Creed, you're lost on day one!

When you abuse your position for sexual favors, better seats at the ball game, to hobnob with the "beautiful people" or the power-brokers; take the stripes off—you have disgraced them.

When you have no issue with sending others into harm's way but you refuse to take your turn; take the stripes off—you have disgraced them.

When you feel that perception trumps evidence; take the stripes off—you have disgraced them.

When you become so politically correct that you're ineffective; take the stripes off—you have disgraced them.

If the only management style you practice is touchy-feely; take the stripes off—you have disgraced them.

If the only management style you practice is hard-ass; take the stripes off—you have disgraced them.

I remember hearing a story about an older Chief. One day his commander came in and said, "Chief," the Colonel said, "I hate to ask you this, but you need to be in the desert six days from now for a 90-day rotation. Can you go?"

With no emotion in his voice or without even looking up, the Chief replied, "I put on my uniform this morning, didn't I?" The Colonel was a little taken back by the Chief's response because he wasn't one to talk in riddles.

The Colonel thought to himself, "Has this veteran of 28 years finally gone off the deep end on me?" The wise old protector of the enlisted corps smiled and began to explain.

"Sir, I made a promise to myself more than 20 years ago that I would only put this uniform on as long as I'm available and ready to do the duty it requires of me."

Some of you will get this story; to many others it will completely escape you. Duty means more than negotiating plum assignments and TDYs for yourself or mooching your way into a suite versus a regular billeting room and mustering all of the goof-off time you can.

It means being part of something that is bigger than you will ever be. It means serving, not being served.

It literally means (as taken from the Chief's Creed) that you:

- cannot be bought; that your word is your bond;
- that you put character above wealth;
- that you have opinions and a will and you are larger than your job;
- and you won't lose your individuality in a crowd;
- you don't hesitate to take chances;
- you are as honest in small things as in great ones;
- you will not compromise with wrong;
- your ambitions are not confined to your own selfish desires and interests;
- you will not say do it "because everybody else does it";
- you are true to your friends through good report and evil report, in adversity as well as prosperity;
- you do not believe that shrewdness, cunning, and hard-headedness are the best qualities for winning success;
- you are not ashamed or afraid to stand for the truth when it is unpopular, who can say "no" with emphasis, although all the world is saying "yes."

If you cannot do all of this and more, take the stripes off, you may have "earned" them, but you don't deserve to disgrace them.

The Chief Master Sergeant Rank Chief's

Induction Certificate [2]

In the late 1950's, The United States Air Force introduced a new super enlisted grade to replace its warrant officers in the United States Air Force. This top enlisted grade came to be titled as "Chief Master Sergeant."

The word chief means, "One who is highest in rank or authority." The word master means, "A teacher or mentor." The word sergeant means, "Any of several ranks of noncommissioned officers, appointed to a rank conferring leadership."

In the 1970's, The United States Air Force Chief Master Sergeants adopted the American Indian chief as their symbol. The Indian chief is the highest member of the tribe. The chief is also a teacher or mentor to the warriors of the tribe. The chief—an elder—was looked on for leadership.

The United States Air Force today only promotes one percent of its enlisted force to the rank of Chief Master Sergeant. Today's chief must be a teacher and mentor, and is looked on for leadership of the enlisted force.

On this _____, the _____ Chiefs' Council has officially inducted this new Chief Master Sergeant into our group.

Chapter Seven:
Being a Command Chief

History

The following is from the US Air Force website, www.AF.mil:

The position of **Command Chief Master Sergeant** (CCM) was renamed in November 1998. Formerly titled **Senior Enlisted Advisor**, Command Chief Master Sergeants serve as senior advisors to commanders at Wing, Numbered Air Force (NAF), Field Operating Agency (FOA), and Major Command (MAJCOM) levels.

In a Joint command, when an Air Force Chief Master Sergeant fills a DoD-nominative Command Senior Enlisted Leader position, that individual is also designated as a Command Chief Master Sergeant.

Command Chiefs advise the Commander on all enlisted matters, including all issues affecting the command's mission and operations, and the readiness, training, utilization, morale, technical and professional development, and quality of life of all enlisted members in the organization.

Command Chiefs are the functional managers for First Sergeants in their entire command/organization. NOTE: Joint Command Senior Enlisted Leader (aka Senior Enlisted Advisor) positions are those that require individuals to hold the following ranks: Army Command Sergeant Major (CSM), Marine Corps Sergeant Major (SgtMaj), Navy Command, Force or Fleet Master Chief Petty Officer (CMDCM, FORCM or FLTCM), Air Force Command Chief Master Sergeant (CCM), or Coast Guard Command Master Chief Petty Officer (MCPO). In order to fill Joint DoD-nominative Joint Command Senior Enlisted Leader positions, each military service nominates one individual to the Joint Commander/Director.

Becoming a Command Chief

I was on a specialized tour with DEA's High Intensity Drug Interdiction Area (HIDIA) when one of my co-workers died. At the funeral, I saw Command Chief Bob Heinrich from the 147th Fighter Wing of the Texas Air National Guard. Half joking, I asked him if he had found a chief's slot for me at Ellington, he nodded.

I said, "We need to talk." At that time I was driving four and a half hours to drill, something I had been doing since 1990. Chief Heinrich and I met after the funeral over coffee.

The position he was talking about was his own, the Command Chief slot.

"Holy Crap, Batman," I thought.

In February of 2000, before I became a Chief Master Sergeant I interviewed for the position of Command Chief at the 147th Tactical Fighter Wing at Ellington Field with the Texas Air National Guard—and I got the job! I made Chief in July and was installed as Command Chief in August.

How It Came About

I had a desire to be a Chief Master Sergeant, but it was vague, like wanting to be the President or something.

I put off completing my Professional Military Education for several years. Heck, I was a Master Sergeant (E-7). I was a First Sergeant. I didn't think it could get any better than that. My wife kept encouraging me to finish the Senior NCO Academy Course and finally I did.

One month later a position opened up and I took off the Diamond and put on E-8; I was a Senior Master Sergeant. All the universe had been waiting on was for me to complete the class.

Two years later I had the time in grade to make Chief Master Sergeant. I was in the correct slot, had all of my "I"s dotted and my "T"s crossed; then WHAM—I nailed Command Chief!

I wish I could tell you I had a brilliant, well executed plan. I didn't. I wish I could tell you it had been a life time goal that through persistence and hard work I attained. It wasn't. I never thought I'd make it because I couldn't see myself as a Chief.

Chiefs walk on water, they glow in the dark, and they can levitate to 3.5 feet! I wasn't like that.

I had never stopped to realize that more than anything else; a Chief Master Sergeant was a person. They weren't born Chiefs, heck prior to 1957 the Air Force didn't even have the rank.

What I'm trying to tell you is that if I had "wanted" to be a Chief I probably could have been one a lot sooner. I didn't even think I was Chief material. Others were seeing things in me I couldn't see in myself.

I had no idea what a Chief did or how they did it. They were simply omnipotent and somehow more competent and confident that the rest of us. In my own mind, I wasn't "good" enough to be a Chief.

Knowing When You're Ready

In my book *Anderson's Rules*, one of the rules I talk about is: You're never ready for anything until you have been in it for a while. The time is different for each person and each task, but six weeks is about right.

Many years ago, I was fortunate to have George King come to my martial arts class. At that time he was 57 and the oldest student I had ever had.

George was in great shape at 57. He was a runner and routinely did half marathons and occasionally a full one. It was he who introduced me to Richard Bach and the book, *Illusions*, a book which had profound impact on me. He is without exception the most "spiritual" man I have ever met. Throughout our entire relationship, he has maintained a "center" that few people ever experience, even for a short time.

When George first came to the class he had that typical "stiffness" that many runners develop. He was only able to properly kick about six inches off the ground. If he went any higher, he'd lose his technique.

Three years later, I was sparring with him and conversing with another student. "Old George" had great hands and you had to watch them, but quite frankly his feet were never a threat, until that day.

While I was conversing I saw George set up for a round house kick and without much thought I blocked about waist level. His foot impacted the right side of my chest and I saw stars. He had kicked at least eight inches higher than he ever had, with perfect technique.

He rushed to see if I was okay and felt tremendous sorrow that he had hurt me. My comment, albeit through clenched teeth and broken breath was, "Good kick, George."

If I have been his Sensei, he has been my Guru, my Messiah. He is a "magician" of the highest order. That simply means, he has both the ability to make magical things happen and see when magic is missing. He is the closest thing I have ever met to Donald Shimodo from *Illusions*.

I find that many people are turned off or fearful of the martial arts; the same way a lot of people are turned off or fearful of the military. They feel karate is "too physical" for them (it is not) and that it teaches you how to fight (it doesn't; it teaches when to fight). It is similar with the military; during and after Vietnam the military was denigrated and maligned.

Honestly, I've known a lot of "hard" men in the military and a couple of "hard" women; I never met a "baby killer" however. I met many that accepted challenges and became better people than they probably would have been without the military; myself included.

I have found that most people seek challenges after having watched from the bleachers. They watch someone else doing something that they think they want to do. The problem is they are watching someone do something they have been doing for a while. That person has practiced and refined their process.

That process may be the military, martial arts, management, sports or just living. It is impossible to see how much time and effort was expended in developing the skills and technique to "make it look easy."

It is impossible to know how many times they failed, how many times they screwed it up. It is impossible to see the effort it took to make the magic. Therefore, when the watcher gets off the bleachers and begins to work the process, it is easy for that person to fail.

It is a lot harder doing something than it is watching. All, or most of the mistakes the doer made, the watcher will probably make as he or she begins to become the doer.

It is only when you move out of the bleachers, off the side line and into the pit where a particular task is performed and you start performing that task; that you understand the intricacies of the task, whatever that task may be.

So often, we hear folks say, "I'm ready for that job, I am ready to become … I am ready to accept …" Ladies and Gentlemen, you are not. The reason is that you've been sitting in the bleachers, on the side lines, in another job or circumstance and all you've seen is that which is visible.

How often have you seen someone pursue a goal, achieve that goal and then fail at the job? The reason? They did not know what else was associated with that job that they could not see. Some things may be intangible; some things may be hidden by the person currently in that job.

This is not to say they were deceived, but maybe the incumbent has spent a long time perfecting his/her abilities in that job. He or she will make it look easy, because they know how to do it.

Want Power

I am in awe of anyone with musical talent. It amazes me to watch folks that can play any instrument and particularly those that play several. I have trouble playing the radio. They make it look so easy. They make it look like fun. They make it look effortless.

Several years ago, I decided I would play the guitar. I struggled, my fingers hurt, by back hurt, my ears hurt (and the ears of those around me hurt). It was not effortless, it was work.

Further it is only after you have been performing the task for a period of time that you can appreciate ALL of the issues involved in it.

By the way, I quit the guitar. I didn't have enough "Want" power.

George wanted to become good at martial arts. For a long time, he could not bend, he could not kick; his movements were stiff and mechanical. He was a dismal failure at most tasks he attempted. He simply could not do many of the things that I required of him.

They say that the bumblebee is physically incapable of flight. Like the bumblebee, George had reasons to fail, but also like the bumblebee, no one ever told him he could not fly. He "wanted" to be successful and he was willing to do those things that were necessary, so he became successful. He could not compete with the younger students. He could only fight himself. He only competed with himself.

He had to make that journey on his own, and he did. While he had support from the class, it was contingent on him to accomplish what he found out was a lot harder than he originally thought. And that is the way it is for all of us.

I found that being a Chief was hard. Even some Chiefs fail at it; they remain simply E-9s.

Was I ready to be a Chief? I didn't think so, even though I had come to want it badly. Evidently the universe thought I was.

Getting Into Position

An interesting side bar to this story. The day that I was promoted to Senior Master Sergeant (E-8) and assumed that position was the day a Master Sergeant retired from the Reserve. Why? Because I took his spot, he wanted to be a Senior. He had been in the slot for several years but had never bothered to finish his Professional Military Education requirements.

He felt he had been wronged. He felt he deserved the promotion, even though he had not done what he needed to do to be eligible for that promotion. He reacted emotionally based on a perceived wrong that had been "done" to him, so he pulled the plug and retired.

He never got the point that the person who had wronged him was himself. Had he bothered to finish the Senior NCO Academy course—he, not me—would have made E-8 and he, not me—would have been set up to make Chief two years later. Emotionally he felt he "deserved" the promotion because he was a nice guy.

A reality check should have shown him that he could not be promoted without that course but he felt entitled to the rank and privileges. No one is entitled to anything they have not earned. He didn't earn the promotion and that was his fault. The bad thing is that we were friends before it occurred.

One of the premises of the Air Guard's Chief Executive Course was to teach new Chiefs how to be Chiefs. After all of the support material, educational activities, etc., it boiled down to this: "Each of us bring our own personalities to the rank. Your job is to do your duty to the best of your ability and when you finally leave the job—if you have made it a little better than it was when you got there—ya done good!"

Problem Wall

In my office as Command Chief, I created the "Problem Wall." It was one of several techniques I used to eliminate the "uniqueness" of an everyday problem. Following are words from one of several plaques I created and had hanging on the wall. When someone came in my office to complain, I sent them to the wall to find the plaque that dealt with their issues.

It always worked.

All You Have to do is Convince Me!

Hold it! It is obvious to me that we are disagreeing on this topic.
That is not necessary.
Are your ideas unlawful, unethical or violate Air Force
Instructions? If so stop now, we will not agree to violate those standards.
However, if that is not the case you have an excellent chance of winning my support.
All you have to do is convince me.
It is obvious to me that you have not managed that, yet.
Why not go back and do some more staff work, develop research that supports your posture, evidence that indicates its probability of success and refine your manner of presentation.
Please do not take this disagreement personally—we are both professionals. Staff work is more important in most cases than passion. However, all of the staff work in the world will never eliminate the need for passion.
But, let us remain professional.
I am not trying to frustrate you—I am waiting to be convinced—you are not there yet. If you remain passionate about this project, try again. I promise to listen.
But I do not promise to agree. My agreement will be based on **how good _you_ do your job.**

All you have to do is convince me.

By Bob Anderson

PART THREE: LEADERSHIP

Chapter Eight:
Leadership: The Good, Bad and the Ugly

I know of few words more misunderstood than leadership. For over 30 years in the military, I heard that leadership comes from the top down. It does not.

Leadership begins where a leader happens to be standing. Certainly a General can issue orders and directives and that is part of leadership, but it is those below the General that actually make those orders and directives function.

It is the same in the corporate world. The Board of Directors or CEO issues orders and directives, but again it is up to those lower on the totem pole to make them work. They (the ones lower on the totem pole) also must display leadership or they will be unable to impact and implement those orders and directives.

By the time that the orders and directives (military or civilian) have filtered down to the lowest levels of the organization, each higher level has had to use leadership effectively.

It is the same for the military or civilian world. It makes no difference if you are talking about a combat unit or a corporation, a school system or a mom and pop store; or a family. You can make demands and issue orders but you can't make anyone else comply. They have to want to comply and they have to be able to comply.

I have heard a lot about "making a team." I don't think you can; you have to build a team.

A manager does things right; a leader does right things. Most of the time, doing the right thing is uncomfortable, anxiety creating and just no fun at all. It makes you unpopular and people won't like you.

Having said all of that, doing anything other than the "right thing" is by its very description NOT the right thing. When you are faced with a "damned if you do and damned if you don't" situation—do what is right.

That is what a leader does.

Management vs. Leadership

Managing, leading and commanding touch on, but do not describe Leadership. You could describe the process as getting people to do what you want them to do, but in this "kinder and gentler" world that sounds too much like Verbal Judo.

You could describe the process as manipulation, negotiation or cooperation. But those words do not cover what I am talking about either. As I mentioned above, I've heard it said that Managers do things right but Leaders do the right thing. So let us begin by calling this process "doing the right thing."

The first thing an effective leader must learn is that some people want to be led. The second thing is some people will be led. The third thing is some people will never be led. Your job is determining which group you're dealing with.

There is a personality of Leadership. Actually, it is more complicated than that—it is really a series of relationships or didactics. There is the didactic between the leader and the person led. There is a relationship between the person led and the leader.

There is a didactic between the person being led and the leader and all of the people watching the process. Finally, there is a didactic between the person being led, the leader, all of the people watching the process and the evaluator of the entire scene.

As I said, some people want to be led. This is a condition that most adults will experience at different times in their lives. I want someone to show me what to do when I am in a circumstance that I am unfamiliar with or untrained for or I am uncomfortable in.

As an NCO I had to learn all of the above and a lot more. One of the most difficult things to learn was "grace." I mean how to appear "graceful" particularly under moments of stress. Chaos breeds chaos and fear multiplies fear. Fear plus chaos limits options and often means death.

Political correctness has added to the difficulties of leadership. Leaders must act; they must lead! When placed in a position of command, command!

A good leader realizes he/she is only part of a team; but he/she is an incredibly important part of that team.

A good leader has to know when and how to be emotional. A good leader has to know when to keep emotions in check. A good leader must be consistent and trustworthy. At the same time, a good leader has to know when and how to motivate each member of his team.

Each member will have their own quirks, abilities and disabilities. A good leader has to know how to motivate each—that means not everyone will respond to the same tactics or approaches.

As General Collin Powell says, "Being responsible sometimes means pissing people off. Good leadership involves responsibility to the welfare of the group, which means that some people will get angry at your actions and decisions. It's inevitable, if you're honorable. Trying to get everyone to like you is a sign of mediocrity: you'll avoid the tough decisions, you'll avoid confronting the people who need to be confronted, and you'll avoid offering differential rewards based on differential performance because some people might get upset."

"Ironically, by procrastinating on the difficult choices, by trying not to get anyone mad, and by treating everyone equally 'nicely' regardless of their contributions, you'll simply ensure that the only people you'll wind up angering are the most creative and productive people in the organization."[1]

As an NCO I developed a less wordy approach, "You have to be willing and able to shoot your own dog!"

I once had a Lt Col tell me that "Officers are leaders and NCOs are managers!" It is a credit to my training that I didn't slap the jackass, but it does show the mind set of many Air Force Officers. This is the same guy I created the Rule of Ego for, it says simply never, ever, ever believe your own BS.

Leadership is the art and science of leading. It is a remarkable process that few people ever truly appreciate. For the past several years there has been a concerted push to replace Leadership with Management and Supervision.

In my never to be humble opinion this is a monumental mistake. Managers do things right, Leaders do right things. Supervisors are mixed in there somewhere, depending on your frame of reference.

Leaders are seldom made, although aspects of leadership can be learned. Most of the time, leaders find themselves in that position. I have only known a few true leaders; and that is as it should be.

These people have the unique ability to draw people to them naturally. These leaders have the unique ability to engender a desire in another person to perform and win the approval of the leader.

There is a terrible responsibility with leadership. A leader can never truly be part of the team. He or she must remain separate yet connected to the team. They must remain the leader.

Can You Shoot Your Own Dog?

In *Anderson's Rules*, I use the analogy of "Ol' Yeller" to teach supervisors and managers how to supervise and manage.

I've received overwhelming response to the concept that doing the right things usually means doing the hard things.

Sometimes, this shows up as "Leadership by Example." The important thing to remember is that it is just as important in our personal life as it is in our professional one. Here is the story of 'Ol Yeller:

'Ol Yeller—by Fred Gipson and Walt Disney

It was in the 1840s, down in the Texas hill country, when the story took place. On a small farm, a family of four had struggled against Indians, weather and hardship to make a life. The father leaves for a three month cattle drive along with the other men in the loosely structured community. His oldest son, Travis, is left to be "the man of the house" in his father's absence.

After the father was gone for a couple of days, a yellow mongrel dog shows up and decides to "adopt the family."

Artis, Travis' brother, loves the dog and begs his older brother to let the dog stay. Begrudgingly, Travis allows the dog to stay. Over the next weeks, the dog becomes a valued pet, and even Travis feels a bond with the dog. They named him Yeller.

One day Travis and Yeller are out in the woods when they are suddenly attacked by wild hogs. Yeller valiantly defends Travis, saving his life. Yeller is seriously injured and Travis, wounded himself, goes for help.

Treated by his mother, Travis refuses to abandon Yeller and insists on going back to get him. With great difficulty, Yeller is brought home and successfully treated. Yeller is fully accepted as part of the family now.

Then, neighbors send word of an outbreak of rabies in the area. Travis and his mother realize one of their cows is infected. Travis shoots the cow and they decide to cremate the body to prevent spread of the disease.

Travis' injuries prevent him from hauling wood, so the mother and a young neighbor girl haul wood and build a bon fire. They continue to haul wood in order to keep the fire going until the body has been consumed.

Suddenly, Travis hears his mother scream for help; Travis grabs his rifle and hobbles to the scene. Travis can see by the light of the bon fire, that Yeller and a wolf are locked in deadly combat. Travis takes aim and fires, killing the wolf. His mother explains the wolf attacked and Yeller saved them.

Travis feels very proud that Yeller is a hero again. Then the mother realizes, "No sane wolf would attack this close to the fire." She suspects the wolf is infected with rabies.

When Travis' mother tells him this and she asks him to shoot Yeller, the boy is devastated. Travis convinces his mother to let him pen up the dog to see if the symptoms of rabies would develop.

After being penned up for a while, Yeller is apparently healthy, and Artis forces the issue to let Yeller out. He opens the door to the pen and slams it shut. Yeller snarls and is foaming at the mouth. He has rabies.

Travis is devastated because now there are no other options. He must act. If he does not act, his friend will suffer a horrible and lengthy death. If he does not act, Yeller could escape and attack a family member, or friend.

Travis' mother offers to shoot Yeller, but Travis says, "No, he's my dog. I'll do it."

In that terrible moment, Travis chose to do a hard thing because it was the right thing to do. While it was not a conscious thing, he demonstrated leadership by example to his younger brother.

In the days and weeks following this terrible incident, Travis chooses to have a positive attitude—he honored Yeller's memory and gathered strength and character from the ordeal.

This is what a leader does. Now, let's look at the similarities found in this story and how they correlate to leadership.

Travis demonstrated good decision making and reasoning when he convinces his mother to let him pen up Yeller. In any tough dilemma, if time allows, we should evaluate the problem before we take action that can't be undone.

When it's determined that Yeller does in fact have rabies, Travis chooses to "hire himself to manage himself," and be accountable and responsible. These are qualities and characteristics that we should use in any dilemma, or professional difficulty.

The answer is simple—hire yourself to manage yourself. Do as good a job for yourself as you would for an employer. Give yourself the same good advice you would give your best friend.

We are all either followers or leaders and we change periodically and episodically in those roles depending on circumstance.

Do you know how people view you? Do people respect you and ask for your advice? Do you listen to what others say and incorporate their ideas to make yourself a better person? Do people take your advice?

Remember, just because you are a manager or supervisor, does not mean you are viewed by others as a leader. Do you stand up for what is right, or are you a "yes" man or woman?

Look again at the title of this section; it does not say, "Do you want to shoot your own dog?" No one wants to have to do that. It reads "Can you shoot your own dog?"

Can you do the hard things that you do not want to do?

Can you take the right path when it is not the easiest path?

Can you do the right thing when it is unpopular?

Can you do your duty even when doing that duty places you in opposition to your friends and colleagues?

Can you do the hard right things that you do not want to do?

Can you shoot your own dog?

A Handful of Leadership

1. Hire yourself to manage yourself.
2. Be accountable and responsible.
3. Lead by example—A leader must stand apart but not alone.
4. Maintain a positive attitude.
5. Be loyal.

Good Examples of Bad Examples

Not everyone can be a good leader. Some people spend an entire lifetime walking around on the face of the earth, going to school, graduating, getting married, having children, working, getting promoted having grandchildren and eventually dying.

Their sole contribution to the world is to be viewed as a good example of a bad example. One of these I will call SSgt "Fat Eddie" Dean (not his real name). Fat Eddie was a piece of work. He tried to get me to go AWOL from basic training. What I didn't know is he had a bounty hunter arrangement with the local cops.

He set up some airman, the Cops would arrest him and Fat Eddie got a bounty! Years later, who shows up to be my Flight Commander—Fat Eddie!

Fat Eddie was the only person in the military I ever refused to work with. He was the only one I would not work with. He was the best example of a bad example I ever saw, but I still learned from him.

Sometimes we learn more from the bad people we encounter than we do from the good ones. Particularly, adult learners seem to put more emphasis on avoidance of negatives than rewarding the positive.

Some of us have wonderful mentors that have a profound and ongoing impact on our life. One of mine was a seventh grade teacher, Mrs. Madeline Miley.

She offered me encouragement, acceptance and praise. I sincerely wanted her respect. She gave me my first "speaking engagement" when I was in the eighth grade.

She invited me back to tell her class about a gift I had made for her. From that moment on, I knew I wanted to be a teacher and a professional speaker.

I now call that realization a "knowing," but that "knowing" was buried under my own fears and inadequacies.

Had I listened to lazy bosses, lazy supervisors, and the emerging politically correct gurus; had I avoided failure, had I not failed, had I not kept learning and perfecting my skills—my life would have been significantly different and you would not be reading these words.

One of the best bosses I ever worked for was a blatant racist and male chauvinist, but he was consistent. That consistency was his saving grace. I would not have wanted to sip good bourbon with him while we discussed the finer aspects of life and philosophy. I would not have wanted to socialize in any format with him, but as a boss—he was great.

He gave good direction and he was willing to confront misbehavior and correct inappropriate behavior. Once I learned his expectations, it was easy to come up to them.

One of the worse bosses I ever had was a brilliant man, a wonderful physician, a great healer but a lousy boss. He had two primary faults. First he tried to appease everyone.

Two people could go into his office at separate times with vastly different and opposing views. Both would leave thinking the commander was in total agreement with each position.

Secondarily, he could not bring himself to confront misbehavior. These two conditions combined to create a situation where subordinates operated in a state of confusion with little, if any, relevant direction and guidance. Everyone loved the guy, nobody want him for a boss.

Both of these men ended up (at least for me) being good examples of bad examples. Had the two been blended together, the result would have probably been the ideal boss.

Let's look at some other individuals whose drive, abilities, education, etc. enabled them to arrive at positions of responsibility and authority; but for some reason, self-destructed or never reached their full potential. We have all seen them.

The first I will describe is the "Salesperson." Everyone loves this guy or gal. They are exciting, dynamic, charismatic, intelligent, usually attractive and even knowledgeable. So what is the problem you ask?

Everyone knows that they are being "worked" by this individual. The level of veracity is challenged by the apparent near total lack of sincerity. This is the kind of person who will give the shirt off his back—provided there is a benefit to him/her.

Then there is the "Hero." This person presents a dynamic and assertive front. Unfortunately, it is only a front. This person's bravado covers a frightened and terrified individual incapable of rising to the circumstances they create.

Invariably this person creates turmoil that someone else has to resolve. They are as dangerous as a loaded gun; not to themselves but to those people who believe the bravado and suddenly find themselves in over their heads.

There was a guy I worked with at Barksdale AFB, LA in the Security Police. He "talked" the best fight you ever heard.

One night we were riding together and I had to apprehend five people. During the confrontation it became necessary to use physical force to make the apprehension. When the fight started, the last time I saw him was as he was running away "to get help."

Another supervisor that ended up being a good example of a bad example was the guy that was an officer, had a MBA, was a leader in his community, but he was an amoral, sociopathic personality that would and did sell me out to cover his own position.

My problem was that I could see the potential in the man. I had never known anyone that could compete with him. I wanted him to be a great leader—I wanted it for him more than he did. I gave him my best and he simply took and took and finally almost destroyed my career, because I let him.

I had another supervisor that one day told me I managed through fear and intimidation. Not only did it shock me, it hurt my feelings. Pondering his comment I realized that if you have confidence and competence, you will of necessity intimidate those around you that have less of either.

Furthermore, there is nothing you can do about it except try to be sensitive to other people's weaknesses.

Earning Respect

I was hired as a Quality Control Supervisor in the mid-eighties. The big boss introduced me and said I had a college degree. Bill Franklin (I've changed his name), said, "Call me Bill."

He was a hard old gentleman with only a high school education; he had pulled himself up to a position of high authority and responsibility by the sweat of his own brow and determination.

One Friday afternoon he called me into his office and read me the riot act. "You are the worst supervisor I have. I don't know why we hired you but if you don't get on board—I'll fire you!!!"

This came as a total shock to me and I could not get him to even tell me what the problems were. Needless to say I had spent better weekends. After much thought I could only come up with one thing I could think of to change.

Monday morning I made that one change. Three weeks later, he called me back into his office and congratulated me on my wonderful transformation, told me I was his best supervisor and when I went up for training director of the plant, he was one of my strongest supporters.

Any idea what I changed? Until the day he died, I never called him Bill again. He was always Mr. Franklin. He needed respect, he felt as though this young "whipper snapper" with a college degree wasn't showing him the proper respect, even though it was him that had set the tenure of our relationship.

Santana said, "Those that do not remember history are destined to repeat it." We must remember our history, our cultural history, the legends and myths of our grandfathers, the wonders of our forefathers.

We must remember so we may warn our children and grandchildren.

I heard a joke once about when NASA was preparing for the Apollo project; they did some astronaut training on a Navajo Indian reservation, it goes like this:

One day, a Navajo elder and his son were herding sheep and came across the space crew. The old man, who spoke only Navajo, asked a question which his son translated. "What are these guys in the big suits doing?"

A member of the crew said they were practicing for their trip to the moon. The old man got all excited and asked if he could send a message to the moon with the astronauts.

Recognizing a promotional opportunity for the spin-doctors, the NASA folks found a tape recorder. After the old man recorded his message, they asked the son to translate it. He refused.

So the NASA reps brought the tape to the reservation where the rest of the tribe listened and laughed but refused to translate the elder's message to the moon.

Finally, the NASA crew called in an official government translator.

He reported that the moon message said, "Watch out for these guys; they have come to steal your land."[2]

"As An NCO Sees It"

In 1967, Sergeant Major John G. Stepanek hit the nail on the head when he wrote *As a Senior NCO Sees It* [3]:

What do we expect from you as officers, commanders, leaders? We expect of you unassailable personal integrity and the highest of morals. We expect you to maintain the highest state of personal appearance.

We expect you to be fair—to be consistent—to have dignity, but not aloofness to have compassion and understanding—to treat each soldier as an individual, with individual problems.

And we expect you to have courage—the courage of your convictions—the courage to stand up and be counted—to defend your men when they have followed your orders, even when your orders were in error—to assume the blame when you are wrong.

We expect you to stick out your chin and say, "This man is worthy of promotion, and I want him promoted." And we expect you to have even greater courage and say, "This man is not qualified and he will be promoted over my dead body!"

Gentlemen, I implore you do not promote a man because he is a nice guy, because he has a wife and five kids, because he has money problems, because he has a bar bill. If he is not capable of performing the duties of his grade, do not do him and us the injustice of advancing him in grade.

When he leaves you, or you leave him, he becomes someone else's problem!

Gentlemen, we expect you to have courage in the face of danger.... During your tour, opportunities will arise for you to display personal courage and leadership.

Opportunities could arise from which you may emerge as heroes. A hero is an individual who is faced with an undesirable situation and employs whatever means at his disposal to make the situation tenable or to nullify or negate it.

Do not display recklessness and expose yourself and your men to unnecessary risks that will reduce their normal chances of survival. This will only shake their confidence in your judgment.

Remember one thing. Very few noncommissioned officers were awarded stripes without showing somebody something, sometime, somewhere. If your platoon sergeant is mediocre, if he is slow to assume responsibility, if he shies away from you, maybe sometime not too long ago someone refused to trust him, someone failed to support his decisions, someone shot him down when he was right. Internal wounds heal slowly; internal scars fade more slowly.

Your orders appointing you as officers in the United States Army appointed you to command. No orders, no letters, no insignia of rank can appoint you as leaders.... Leaders are made, they are not born. Leadership is developed within yourselves.

You do not wear leadership on your sleeves, on your shoulders, on your caps, or on your calling cards. Be you lieutenants or generals, we're the guys you've got to convince and we'll meet you more than halfway.

You are leaders in an Army in which we have served for so many years, and you will help us defend the country we have loved for so many years. I wish you happiness, luck, and success in the exciting and challenging years that lie ahead. May God bless you all!

———————

"The Choice of NCO's…"

Major General Friedrich Baron Von Steuben said in 1779, "The choice of non-commissioned officers is an object of the greatest importance: The order and discipline of a regiment depends so much upon their behaviour, that too much care cannot be taken in preferring none to that trust but those who by their merit and good conduct are entitled to it. Honesty, sobriety, and a remarkable attention to every point of duty, with a neatness in their dress, are indispensable requisites; a spirit to command respect and obedience from the men, an expertness in performing every part of the exercise, and an ability to teach it, are absolutely necessary, nor can a sergeant or corporal be said to be qualified who does not write and read in a tolerable manner."[4]

"Building a NCO"

J. D. Pendry in his *Building a NCO: Setting the Foundation* wrote, "Major General Von Steuben wrote the prescription for noncommissioned officers when our nation and Army were in desperate need of professional soldiers and leaders. He knew that an army of citizen soldiers required professional noncommissioned officer leadership for it to succeed against the well-trained super power of the day."

"It's Difficult to be a Good NCO"

Former Sergeant Major of the Army Connelly said, "It is difficult to be a good noncommissioned officer. If it had been easy, they would have given it to the officer's corps."[5]

The Army Study Guide identifies that the NCO in America's fledgling Continental Army came about through a combination of factors. "America's NCO corps just didn't happen. It evolved over the years, tapping ideas and innovations from many different sources."

"The first NCOs or relatives of the breed were probably those exceptional legionaries serving Rome's empire. They commanded 10 soldiers while assisting their commander in handling his 100 men. These legionaries supervised training, performing administrative and logistical support tasks as they arose."[6]

Anderson's Rule of Large Numbers

I don't know very many people that get up in the morning with the attitude of, "Hey, let's see how bad I can screw up my life today." I don't know very many people that wake up and decide, "I've got a great idea, let's see if I can get fired today."

I don't know very many people that get up and decide, "You know, I think I'll see if I can destroy my family today," but believe it or not, there are some.

In *Anderson's Rules*, I talk about how most folks shy away from unneeded turmoil in their life. Most folks want to do "good" and most will do "good," if they know what "good" looks like. Some folks need a little more help to become functionally adept at their job, their career, and their familial responsibilities.

They are not trying to mess up; they probably just don't have a clear view of what "good" looks like.

I see this often in business and industry as well as in the military. The officer or boss gets frustrated and decides to fire an employee or write up a troop that is not measuring up. I don't have a problem with that.

What I have a problem with is when the officer or boss never developed the troop or employee, never showed that person what they expected. I have a problem when a supervisor does not give feedback to a troop or employee so they can correct mistakes or shortcomings.

For years I have dealt with employees and troops that had received no job descriptions. I've seen too many troops and employees that have never had a performance evaluation and believed they are doing their job well—until the day they are fired or got written up.

Supervisors and managers need to "parent" their subordinates. It is like dealing with your children. The child who is told, "Clean up your room" may pick up five toys and feel they have done exactly what the parent wanted.

If the parent means "pick up every toy and vacuum the room," that parent needs to convey that message in terms the child can understand. The same is true of supervisors and managers.

If we want something from someone else, we must be clear in setting correct expectations, AND we must have agreement on those expectations from both parties. This holds true in most of our dealings.

I have used Anderson's Rule of Large Numbers for over twenty years, to teach managers and supervisors a particular point. Specifically, Anderson's Rule of Large Numbers says that 85% of your people will give you their very best the very first time. 10% will require more training and more guidance but they also will perform well.

That leaves five percent. Of that five, three percent of the people will try your patience and require extraordinary efforts in the areas of communications and boundary setting, but will be successful if enough effort is exerted.

They are difficult to direct, but when they get it—THEY GOT IT. They will be your elite. They have enough courage to challenge the system. They will not just be successful—they will be highly successful. They will excel.

The remaining two percent will never function in accordance with standards, boundaries or expectations. You will need to just shoot them and be done with it. They, for some reason, have made the conscious decision NOT to be successful and they will not allow you to make them successful.

Their disobedience, their criminal behavior, their unethical behavior, their cheating behavior—are all patterns that will be enforced by their personality. They will walk across the street in the rain to screw up, when they could stay indoors and be successful.

The job of an effective leader, supervisor, manager, etc. is not to handle the first 85%, they will handle themselves. It is not to handle the next 10%, they just need a little help and that is usually an easy task.

Their job is to tell the difference between the last three and two percent. Only then can they focus on providing the guidance that the three percent need to be outstanding and excel, and stop wasting time on the incorrigible two percent that have chosen to fail.

"A Manager manages things. A Leader leads people. A Manager does things right. A Leader does right things." —Author Unknown.

1st Corollary to Anderson's Rule of Large Numbers

If you took a group made up entirely of three percenters (the absolute elite, according to Anderson's Rule of Large Numbers) within six weeks, that group will have started to stratify itself. You will end up with aberrant behavior, misbehavior and failure at the two percent level. You will have three percent of the population exceed at entirely new levels; and the 10% and 85% groups will have reestablished themselves.

Bottom line, regardless of the group, the rule always holds true.

2nd Corollary to Anderson's Rule of Large Numbers

The difference between three percenters and two percenters is this: Three percenters will screw stuff up trying to make something happen. Two percenters will screw stuff up insuring nothing happens. Both are equally adept at justifying their actions. The three percent will justify their EXPLANATIONS while the two percent will justify their EXCUSES.

Chapter Nine:
Following Instructions

Part of leading is following. It is a time honored military adage that if you can't follow, you'll never be a good leader.

Leaders are tasked with following instructions and/or procedures. Instructions or procedures are received from higher authority. They are determined to be non-negotiable. This status will remain unless and until higher authority has amended their position.

Many of the leader's responsibilities are not defined by definitive instructions; they are based in the judgment of the specific leader.

Should a person disagree with an instruction or procedure, it is that person's responsibility to initiate the negotiation. If unable to arrive at a new position—the instruction should be followed as directed. That same process holds true for a subordinate that disagrees with a manager's decision.

This is an important doctrine to get: **Unless a new instruction/directive has been agreed upon—the old instruction/directive remains in effect.**

Should a supervisor/individual disagree with an instruction or procedure, it is that person's responsibility to initiate the negotiation. If unable to arrive at a new position—the instruction should be followed as directed.

That same process holds true for a subordinate that disagrees with a superior's decision.

The bottom line is, **unless a new instruction/directive has been agreed upon—the old instruction/directive remains in effect.**

At that point, the individual must make one of the following decisions:

1. Comply with the instruction,
2. Comply with the instruction and continue to attempt change,
3. Elect not to comply and suffer the consequences,
4. Remove him/herself from the organization.

For that person's supervisor, enforcement of the instruction/direction may involve discipline up to and including termination. Discussion may not be appropriate.

Discussion may not be profitable. This is an application of the fifth rule—**some things are not and should not be negotiated.**

Supervisors are encouraged to listen to subordinates. In many cases, better ideas come from those individuals actually doing the job, instead of those directing it.

However, many solutions expressed by subordinates cannot be implemented due to cost or other factors.

Again, **unless a new instruction/directive has been agreed upon—the old instruction/directive remains in effect.**

In this scenario, the supervisor's ability to negotiate may be limited by factors beyond their control. Likewise, the supervisor's ability to avoid potential disciplinary actions may be limited by the subordinate's attitude and the supervisor's judgment.

Not every suggestion can be implemented—nor should they.

Supervisors should not shift responsibility by statements such as "I agree with you but management is forcing this down our throats." Such statements weaken the supervisor's position of authority and encourage "peering down."

"Peering down" is a by-product of former management styles that advocated management by consensus. Consensus is fine, provided that supervisors are capable of standing hard on issues where consensus is not arrived at.

Supervisors should encourage team efforts and teamwork, provided they remember that by virtue of their job they can never be part of the team in the sense that other employees are. Their job requires the ability to direct, enforce and discipline.

This requires specific skills and duties different from other employees. That is why it is difficult to move from employee status to supervisor status and supervise individuals that were your peers.

The aspect of "being able to shoot your own dog" should be the first point of training for new supervisors. It is hard to be a supervisor and part of that process involves corrective actions and discipline of subordinates.

Can you do the hard things?

Anderson's 5 R's

From first line supervisors through all ranks of management, the qualifier should not be whether or not that person can "do the job of employee" it should be whether or not that person can get the employees to do their jobs.

Not all good employees or troops make good supervisors.

Supervisors with an understanding of the duties of labor make better supervisors. But people with strong labor concepts, ties and orientation do not usually make good supervisors.

The employee is hired to do a specific job. Unfortunately, most employees do not know what that involves. They have one view of what their job entails and management has another. This is a result of the initial negotiation that occurred when the employee was hired. It is a prime example of typical management operations.

When management and employees agree to those expectations as being within their experience/abilities and they have identified clear expectations—positive and appropriate negotiations were conducted.

Should the employee fail to meet those standards, supervisors are encouraged to utilize the **Five Rs**. At any time a problem employee has been identified, one or more of these should be employed.

1. Re-educate: As previously stated most folks do not have clear understanding of what their job responsibilities are. Re-education by a competent supervisor is essential and usually effective.

2. Re-motivate: Often overlooked, a person will experience a degree of loss of motivation upon learning that what they have been doing is incorrect. Care should be taken to make corrective actions as positive as the situation will allow.

3. Re-design the system: As stated previously, the person doing the job may have figured a more effective and efficient way to do it. Listen and evaluate.

Many great ideas are buried upon the tombstones of "That's the way we have always done it." Or, "We tried that years ago and it did not work." Technology can be improved and not every employee operates at the same level of ability.

In fact, a supervisor may go through these three several times before effective resolution occurs. There is no magic number as to how many times a supervisor should roll one, two and three around.

One supervisor may do it twice, another six times and another sixteen times. It is that SUPERVISOR's judgment and experience that sets the number, but after that number has been reached and the problem continues, then;

4. Re-place the person: On occasion, no resolution will occur and a problem employee still exists. At that point in time, replacement may become necessary. However, if that decision is made, the supervisor may not be allowed to replace the employee because she is the Boss's daughter, the Boss's buddy or some other equally inane reason.

5. Re-sign: At that point, get out of there before you become as crazy as these people are.

It Takes Both Parties

When we are striving for compliance, both parties have responsibilities. Supervisors must set clear expectations. Employees must evaluate their abilities to meet those expectations.

When clear expectations are presented and a valued decision is made that those expectations are within the parameters of the employee's abilities, it becomes the employee's responsibility to meet those expectations—unless or until those expectations are re-negotiated.

Negotiation is only another term for problem-solving. New systems possess capabilities that old systems lacked. With knowledge of new possibilities, rules and regulations, an effective negotiator can recognize that re-designing the system can solve the problems presented by the other side.

The trick is not convincing someone to buy what you are selling. It is telling someone the features and benefits of a system that will solve ALL of their problems. Financial expenditure is always a consideration. Here's a tip.

Leaders should figure that their time and the time of their troops have a dollar value. Additionally, time wasted has emotional value. If a system is not sufficient for the task, people will spend time (add up the hours spent and multiply by an average wage).

Wasted time or repeated efforts mount up quickly. Time investment in a new system costs money. Comparison with the new system's impact on operations, client relations, lost business and frustration for both the client manager and the employees become an effective tool.

The focus of the compensation process is problem-solving. Listening, evaluation and presentation are the essential steps in the process. Compensation negotiations rarely occur with immediate results.

This is often a process that requires additional research on the part of the negotiator to determine which items need to be re-designed in order to resolve the problem while maintaining the unit's (or corporations) available financial and emotional budget.

The more knowledge the negotiator person possesses, the less time spent in research; therefore, the deal is closed more rapidly.

Features and benefits are, and have been the essential factors in the selling process since ancient history. New buzzwords come and go but application of features and benefits remains the core process of effective sales. The same is true for negotiations, because negotiations are the sales process.

I heard a story that makes the point well, it says, "Everyday a gazelle wakes up and has to outrun the fastest lion, or he will be eaten. Everyday a lion wakes up and has to outrun the slowest gazelle, or he will starve. The moral: no matter if you are a gazelle or a lion, when you wake up you'd better be running."[1]

> "In the social order in which one person is officially subordinate to another; the latter (if a gentleman) never mentions it – and the former (if a gentleman) never forgets it."
>
> —Major General "Blackjack" Pershing

The Art of Followership
By Bob Gaylor, Fifth Chief Master Sergeant of the Air Force
(Reprinted by permission, article written in 1979)

Aristotle that famous Greek Chief Master Sergeant, once remarked, "One who has not learned to follow can never lead." It might very well be the smartest thing the great philosopher ever said. It is without question a true statement and one we all need to consider and reflect on for a moment. I travel all over the Air Force world giving talks on leadership, but I've often thought that I need to develop a pitch on how to follow. That's where leadership begins.

Is there a difference between the art of following and the art of leading? An Air Force Captain who teaches an off-duty college course in leadership told me he once split his class into two groups. He asked one group to develop a list of favorable leader qualities, and the other a list of favorable follower qualities. He was somewhat surprised to find the lists were almost identical. Traits like loyalty, motivation, self-discipline, honest, aggressiveness, communicative skill, concern for others and initiative appeared on both lists. Are you surprised?

Everyone in the Air Force works for someone so we all qualify as followers. Let's ask ourselves the question, "What do I want from my boss?" I can't answer for you but I can answer for myself. See how many of my points you agree with:

- I want to be treated with respect and human concern. Since those are two-way streets, I have to be respectful toward my boss.
- I don't want preferential treatment but I expect just and fair play. I have to be fair and honest with my boss to earn equality in return.
- I want work that is meaningful and challenging. I've got to show my boss that I possess the skill and training necessary to do my assigned job.
- I want enough authority to make decisions and become involved in planning and organizing my work. It's important that I don't abuse and misuse the authority I'm given.
- I want my boss to communicate, listen and keep me informed. My responsibility is to keep my boss advised of problems and solutions that I might be aware of and to promote open lines of communication.

- I want a boss who inspires me—one who can bring out the best in me. I have to display self-discipline and motivation so my boss will know I'm receptive to instructions and capable of innovation.
- I want a boss who is not impulsive—one who does not act in haste. I have got to show that I can obey rules and standards so I don't place the boss in a compromising position.

One point becomes crystal clear. The relationship between a leader and a follower is a two-way street—a give and take. You cannot be an effective leader or follower unless you do what you can to promote that type of agreement.

Discuss my points with your boss/worker and see how your relationship measures up.

(See the Biographical section to view Bob Gaylor's biographical information).

"What! What men, dodging this way for single bullets! What will you do when they open fire along the whole line? I am ashamed of you. They couldn't hit an elephant at this distance." A few seconds after, a man who had been separated from his regiment passed directly in front of the general, and at the same moment a sharp-shooter's bullet passed with a long shrill whistle very close, and the soldier, who was then just in front of the general, dodged to the ground. The general touched him gently with his foot, and said, "Why, my man, I am ashamed of you, dodging that way," and repeated the remark, "They couldn't hit an elephant at this distance."[2]

—General John Sedgwick

Chapter Ten:
My Last Commander

Captain Layne Wroblewski was my Commander at the 917th Security Forces Squadron and (as far as I'm concerned) my last Commanding Officer. Not since 1978 had I heard anyone even approach the philosophies of Col (Ret) Dave Bond (who I'll talk about later); this guy did it and did it in spades.

As soon as he started talking I was hooked.

Over the next two years he proved to me over and over again it was not just talk. He meant it! I had never seen a greater dedication to duty, especially from such (at that time) a young officer.

Captain Wroblewski however, had the benefit of being a Mustang. That means he was formerly enlisted. He knew the game from both sides. He set the standards for physical fitness and being "sharp."

He taught me things I didn't know. He pushed me to be better just to keep up with him. With over a twenty year difference in our ages, it was a chore.

He listened well and genuinely cared for our "kids." He understood what an officer should be and was dedicated to being that. He was both fair and consistent in dealing with the "misbehavior" of some of the troops and consistently went out of his way to watch out for their welfare.

Hard headed, but not to a fault. I personally loved that he "practiced being unreasonable," he made our troops better cops. There is no doubt in my mind that his leadership style saved lives.

I personally think the best compliment an NCO can give to an officer is to say, "I'd go to war with him." Well, I did go to war with him.

One day we were at Silver Flag training before we deployed to Iraq. We were watching a K-9 demonstration. The young Captain was feeling pretty cocky that day (I like cocky). He pulled a ten dollar bill out and said, "Chief, I've got a ten that says you won't 'catch' a dog." That means put the sleeve on and let the dog attack!

I smiled and said, "Is that a fact young Captain. You got a bet." The instructor gave me the sleeve and the dog fight was on. When they called the dog off, I walked over and with a smile removed the ten bucks. The Captain never would get that "old age and treachery will always defeat youth and enthusiasm." I had caught dogs before he was out of diapers, though it had been awhile.

But here's what I loved about him. I held up the ten and said, "Sir, I've got a ten that says you won't catch a dog." He squared his shoulders and took the sleeve from me and caught his dog... and I had plans for that ten!

Response from Last Commander
By former Captain, now Major Layne Wroblewski

One of my favorite pearls of experience involved a relationship I had with my Chief. We had a standard setup—we had a Chief Enlisted Advisor, a First Sergeant, and a newly minted butter-bar. Immediately beneath the Chief were two senior NCOs who were responsible for training and operations, respectively.

I hired the Chief, First Sergeant, and Lieutenant personally. I made a point to encourage creative out of the box thinking. I impressed on all three how critical I felt it was to be surrounded by men who were not yes men but instead brought the devil's advocate, the fresh eyes perspective.

Most importantly, however, was that after the dust settled we had a unified approach to our position. This methodology proved to be the greatest mentoring opportunity I ever had.

The Chief was an old-school bald-headed boozer who smoked cigars like an 18-wheeler billowing exhaust. His demeanor was matter-of-fact—what you saw is what you got. He didn't believe in polishing a turd. "The baby's ugly and we have to work with what we have" was a phrase he used with me regularly.

I remember being startled when I approached my boss telling him I was hiring him. "Why would you hire someone who bucked against a one-star?" I was somewhat alarmed. I just presented my new boss with a decision I was about to make. I was initially nervous that he did not agree with my analysis of the situation.

I was always told that first impressions are lasting impressions, so I thought to myself I had to get this right. Simultaneously I struggled to hold back how excited

I was that this very question immediately validated what I was getting with hiring the Chief.

I expressed that the Chief came very respected among the men and women working for me. I had an immediate imprint of trust and confidence in him. I also gleaned from the conversation with the boss that it would be difficult to change his opinion. As we discussed the hiring decision I concluded that I likely wouldn't change his impression. I worried about the credit I was using with my new boss knowing that I didn't really know the Chief, the Colonel, or their history very well. So I told him I would ponder it.

I called the Chief to discuss the issue. He didn't skirt the issue. He immediately provided facts and promptly told me in a professional manner that if I had any doubt about him that I shouldn't hire him. Again convinced I made a good decision I pressed forward and announced to my squadron my hiring decision. I'll add more about that decision later.

The warriors embraced the Chief and quickly made him a part of the team. The Chief went right to work unpacking issues and providing constructive solutions. He became the confidant several of the troops never had.

I was encouraged with how well the Chief was able to make things happen. But that's a small part of the big gain I had with him on my team.

Many nights the Chief and I would get together over our poisons. His was Jack and 7Up—mine was Crown and Coke. I had two-glasses with a twelve-pack of soft drinks and fifths of each concoction.

We hoped to maintain the ice in the fridge back at the unit as we were only there during drill weekends. The business of leading took place after hours.

The Chief had a popular hangout owned by one of his friends that he and I regularly frequented. The Tiki lounge was just outside of the base and became the meeting spot after work on Saturdays.

I would bring my wife Brooke with me as my squadron was six-hours away from home. It would be a time for her to scrap book while I spent time developing my Lieutenant and getting developed myself by my Chief.

I was a newly minted captain not even out of my thirties and I had received my first command opportunity. It was by far the best job I ever had. The Chief and I would get together at the Tiki Lounge or even in my office while he smoked his life away discussing life.

On many occasions the Chief and I solved the world's problems with those cigars and poison. I learned to lean on him both in my military world and my personal life. We talked like girls on the phone every day. He lived in Houston while I lived in Oklahoma City.

He had become a father to me, a brother to me—a comrade. It was because of this relationship that I learned some of the best leadership traits I ever developed.

The Chief gave me exactly what I asked for. He always saw a different way, an alternative approach to the challenges I was tasked with solving. I knew I had to lead but confided in those three-men to make tough calls. Although I had no problem making a command decision with no input, I felt it was studious to consult with these guys and get input.

The best input would later come from the Chief who had no problem telling me how he felt about any particular topic. The Chief developed a reputation that when he said, "Come on—let's take a drive" you knew he was pissed.

I sat in that Dodge I don't know how many times when he would tell me how he felt about a particular subject. Many times the Chief and I butted heads. We had a common leadership trait in that we both were expressive.

We often talked first and then thought which frequently brought its own challenges. The great leadership trait I gleaned from him, though, was his ability to cycle through his anger and frustration with me, express it, and completely and unilaterally support me.

At first I was taken aback by his "ballsiness," about his ability to confront an issue without concern for my rank or his. However, I remembered that I hired him for this brashness.

I quickly learned to enjoy these conversations as I felt they sharpened my saw. I admired him that he wasn't afraid of me or my capability but instead saw me as a leadership project that he had unfettered access to mold, develop, and cultivate. That is not to say that he did not respect my rank and authority—he emulated what it means to be a servant leader.

The lesson learned here is to surround yourself with other leaders. Search for leaders who outshine you, outsmart you, and think ahead of you. You should have men and women who possess (and regularly demonstrate) exceptional courage and unwavering commitment.

I have applied this trait in my civilian job and hired people who are smarter than me and have their own ideas that are not necessarily the status quo. More importantly, though, is that they are game changers—they are not afraid to disagree with the boss but support the leader in public.

You will find that the best leaders never got to where they were without the help of others. Leaders don't grow on trees—current leaders seek them out and work to make them great leaders.

Our leadership project in our squadron ended as he retired and I chose a different path. But the journey—the experience between the two of us—was only beginning.

And remember the conversation I had with the boss about the Chief? Turns out the Colonel never changed his mind. But it did not matter. The Chief likes to say that "There's nothing more successful in life than living successfully." The impression, the relationship, and the impact I have as a result of hiring the Chief trumps any hesitation I made about impressing the boss. The truth is sometimes you have to respectfully disagree with the boss to be successful.

The Chief is still the singularly most impressive man in my professional and personal life since my father passed. I have not seen him in years, but I talk to him almost every week—and still continue to get that mentoring. Everyone should have a mentor like MY Chief. My life is much more satisfying as a result.

Cap, I'd go to war with you again.
    —Chief

————————————

The Rest of the Story

Now I'm going to tell a little about the rest of the story about my last Commander. As I have mentioned, the Captain is now a Major. He's also now a father of three children. Here's a story that he is too much of an officer and gentleman to tell. The reasons I'm telling it is because it involved me and it is one that should be told.

Wroblewski was more loyal to his men than they were to him. He gave them more than several of them deserved, and it cost him. At a time when we were at war and in Iraq, he was sabotaged by a few scumbags. Not only were some of the scumbags his own troops some were his superiors. One Colonel in particular comes to mind.

Wroblewski served twice in the "sand box." The Colonel never did. Wroblewski commanded troops. The Colonel demanded respect. Wroblewski went into harm's way because it was his duty. The Colonel did his duty from behind a desk, safe stateside. Wroblewski pushed troops. The Colonel pushed paperwork.

Personally, while I always treated that Colonel respectfully; I did not and do not respect him. The NCO Corps has a moral and official job to mentor. Most of the time, I've seen the Officer Corps eat their own.

They didn't get to eat my Captain. He has succeeded and been promoted, showing he has skills and abilities not limited to the profession of arms. He won and by God, I'm going to say it.

Chapter Eleven:
A Word to Officers

Dave Bond—The Best of the Best

I reported to the 97th Security Police Squadron at Blytheville Air Force Base, Arkansas in 1976; the Commander was a young Major by the name of Dave Bond. Major Bond was the closest thing to King Arthur I had ever seen.

Over the next 18 months, we forged an Officer/NCO relationship that was complicated and dynamic. We also forged a friendship that has lasted ever since.

In 1978, he created one of the first Air Force Counter Terrorism Teams and called it the Tactical Neutralization Team (TNT). He told me I should get on it. I told him I had a fear of heights and wasn't jumping out of a helicopter. He told me I wouldn't have to do that because he didn't have any choppers; so I joined.

After we had gone through training there was a graduation exercise. We split the Team into two groups. Our missions were to sweep in, clear the Arms Range area and make contact with the aggressors who were holding hostages.

I had command of the second unit. The first unit had been "wiped out" by trying a dynamic charge across the open ground.

When time came I pulled my team together and gave assignments for each phase of the operation. I had a TSgt named John Loft (I changed the name), he was a fast burner and hard charger and had made quite a name for himself.

I assigned TSgt Loft as an over watch while the team and I cleared the Arms Range. During the second phase someone plopped down next to me. It was Loft! I asked him what he was doing and why he wasn't on over watch.

"Nothing happening there, I want in on the action."

Luckily there were no aggressors at the Range and we moved to the last phase—contact with the enemy.

I knew a charge wasn't going to work any better for my men than it had for the first team. I placed two men (one of them Loft) on opposite sides of a break in the berm.

I told them, "All I want you two to do is fire shots from behind, cover and alternate shooting high and then low. Just stick your rifles around the cover and keep popping off shots high and low."

I took the rest of the team and we low crawled 100 yards or so. When we were within a few feet of the terrorist location, we moved in and "killed" all of the bad guys and rescued the hostages.

The next day, Major Bond called me into his office and told me he wanted me to command the TNT. I was shocked but very pleased, but I knew there was a problem.

"Sir, I'm honored," I said. "But there is a problem." I told him what Loft had done. "I can't take command of the team if he is on it. First of all, he outranks me." I was a SSgt that would be commanding a TSgt.

"Secondly, I don't trust him Sir and I won't put the rest of the team in danger for a 'hot dog.'"

Bond did something I would have never expected and had not seen done before. He moved Loft off the team and put me in charge.

I had a couple of Sergeants that militarily outranked me still on the team. Militarily we served in the Squadron and I was subordinate to them. Operationally, when the team was activated, I was in charge. We never had an issue. They, unlike Loft, were professionals, there to perform a mission.

It would have been very easy for the Major to follow customs; but he knew what we were being tasked with exceeded normal Security Police duties and protocol.

That team ended up being the only one in the Air Force that had an organic Hostage Negotiations Team and were not all Cops. Several were from other organizations and they had to go through the same training we did, minus weapons training.

During my active duty service of ten years, six months and 12 days, I never met another officer like Dave Bond. He retired in 1992 as a full Colonel. During his career he was sent to seven squadrons that were broken, so that he could fix them. Each unit made Best in Air Force the next year.

(See the Biographical section to view Dave Bond's biographical information).

> "Most NCOs accept, as an unwritten duty, the responsibility to instruct novice second lieutenants but they do so only when the student is willing." —Col Griffin N. Dodge

A Letter to Officers

By Bob Anderson

You are a Commissioned Officer in the United States military. As such, you occupy a position of trust, responsibility and respect. Any officer may expect subordinates to respect their rank and position. I challenge you to earn their respect not only for what you are, but also for WHO you are.

By virtue of your rank and position, my duty is to follow your orders. One day, you may order me to attempt something that both of us realize may be impossible.

Both of us may realize that to attempt to follow that order can and probably will result in my men and women making the ultimate sacrifice. But that is our duty and each of us realized that when we swore the oath that placed us under your command.

I did not swear my life and the welfare of my family to a manager. I did not place my family or myself in this position to work for a supervisor. I am deeply committed to serve my country as a member of my country's military defense force. I came to serve my country through the lawful orders of those officers appointed over me.

I came to serve a Leader. Being an officer requires accomplishment. It means you have met the mark, intellectually, academically and through training. But being an officer does not mean you are a Leader. A Leader leads; it is as simple as that.

I have served under officers, managers and supervisors. I have also been fortunate enough to serve under Leaders. For these people, I have been prepared to do whatever is required of me to defend my country—whatever is required.

These people have earned my undying respect and loyalty; not because of a piece of metal on their collar or sleeve, but because of the strength, good judgment and ethic in their hearts. I salute your rank; I follow the person who leads. You may ask me for my health, my life and the lives of the people under me. That is both your right and your duty.

I ask you not to spend us in vain. But I ask that as of today, you to honor our relationship as I do. Do your absolute best for us; we will give you the same. If the ultimate sacrifice is required of me, I ask that you be able to face my family with honor and tell them my sacrifice was not in vain.

If that sacrifice is required of you, on my honor I will stand over you and offer a final salute; not to the tin on your collar, but to an Officer, to a Leader.

—Chief

Appropriately Inappropriate

There are times when a good NCO has to be appropriately inappropriate or respectfully disrespectful with an officer. It is an art not a science. You have to have great confidence in that officer and great trust. Trust is not given, it is earned.

One of the officers I trusted was Lt Col Christopher Culliton. Lt Col Culliton was approaching his retirement and I called and asked for some bullet points to draft an award for him; the Meritorious Service Medal.

Culliton told me, "I haven't done anything for the award" and declined to give me the bullet points. Even though he was a leader in the Squadron and one of those folks that could always be counted on, he thought he was just "doing" his job. The more I thought about it, the madder I got.

I called him back and emailed him, saying:

As I pondered your response I decided to write a couple of thoughts down.

Let me tell you something Sir, we don't get to pick where we serve. We don't get to pick what we get to do as we serve; we don't get to be where we want to be when we serve.

We don't get to decide if we'll live as we serve; we don't get to decide how we'll die if we serve. We don't get to pick when we leave our family as we serve, we don't get to pick what will happen to them while we serve.

We don't get to decide where Thanksgiving Dinner or Christmas Dinner will be served or where Birthday Cake will be served.

We don't get to pick who we will serve with or who we serve under.

We don't get to make all of our decisions as we serve. We don't get to protect ourselves from dumb ones as we serve or determine our lives as we serve. We don't get to decide very much.

For a GI, there are few decisions, we can decide between bad scrambled eggs and bad fried eggs. We can decide between being overworked or the mission failing. We can decide to let people further their own goals or we can stand up and protect our people while they protect our country.

We can decide to get up or face the consequences, we can decide to obey or face the consequences.

There is not a lot that is positive about serving your country. It is hard, it is lonely, it can be cold, it can be hot, it can be rainy or all three.

Some do a few years, and they have done their duty. Some stay a long time, they have done theirs. Some make every moment of their service ugly for themselves, some make every moment of their service ugly for others.

There are others that are beacons during their service. They are often irascible. They are often mavericks. They are often pranksters. They are often politically incorrect. They are often funny. They are often above the turmoil, especially when they are in it.

But they are never petty, they are part of this club, they are the matrix of this club. They hold it together for the rest of us. They are the examples of what we all ought to do but usually do not.

They are people like you.

We don't get to pick where and when we serve; we don't get to pick a hell of a lot. In fact, I guess there are only two things we can pick:

1. Do we serve
2. How we serve

You chose to serve and you have served well. I don't know why you came in, but I'm glad you did. You have touched a lot of folks, me included. You made it better than it was when you got here, not everyone does.

In a moment of chaos, men and women rise up to do great and wonderful things. In long moments and days of turmoil, stupidity and silliness, others most often falter. Others become petty and mean. Others lose their desire to serve.

You did not. You stuck. You never lost your sense of humor or your sense of duty. No, you did not lead people in righteous battle against a terrible foe. No, you did not go and do the fun and exciting things that we all want to do.

You stuck. You did what was asked of you, and then exceeded those expectations. You stuck. You were always there. You did your job and you did it well. You did it without seeking personal gain. You maintained a balance of work, duty and family. When you could have been the commander, you decided to be a great Doc, a good Dad and husband.

Don't you ever say "I haven't done crap" in my presence again. I'll kick your butt. You will not dishonor your service in my presence. It's okay to be humble. You and I know we haven't had it as hard as our brothers and sisters. Some of them came back wounded, some did not come back.

As it says on the T shirt, "Some gave all, ALL gave some." You gave a bunch. Maybe you can't see what you gave. That's fine, you don't need to.

I see! Others see!

Your discharge will simply say Honorable. There is no outstanding discharge. There is only Honorable, there is nothing higher than that. That is what Dwight D. Eisenhower's, General Westmoreland and Audie Murphy's said.

That's what my dad's said and he was awarded the Silver Star. Honorable, such a simple word. Private Snuffy can earn that word, I can earn that word, you have earned that word.

John Wayne never earned that Honorable Discharge and neither did Sylvester Stallone. The two greatest movie war heroes of two generations never served. One had flat feet and the other went to Canada. Both made fortunes portraying what our brothers and sisters did.

Now write the damn bullet points and for one time in your career stand up, shut up and accept the acknowledgements that are due you. Accept them with the same humor and service that has marked your career. Go out well.

Author's Note: Lt Col Culliton received both a Meritorious Service Medal and a Blade of Honor (which I'll tell you about in a later chapter).

A Matter of Mentorship
By Lt Col Culliton, USAFR (Ret)

The thought, the topic of officer/enlisted points brought many things to mind. The evolution or journey in military life is a matter of mentorship. All of us have been mentored or shaped by family, parents, friends, employment, or religion.

What it boils down to is the good luck or grace to have been touched by the example of good mentors; and pass it forward keeping our weaknesses to ourselves and offering our courage to others.

Thoughts determine actions. Actions determine habits. Habits determine character and strength of character determines destiny. The raw material that we bring to military life is honed and refined every day. This requires perseverance and mental toughness.

Dedication to a goal, adherence to an internal standard or code of conduct and the willingness to preserve in an organization that seems to foster mediocrity.

From the first day of basic training, the leveling efforts of the military mindset evens the playing field separating those who don't want to play by the rules or never even had any rules. The cruel reality of ordering people into harm's way and the dull boring monotony require a strong steady focus on the ultimate goal and mission.

The example of good mentors and commanders is essential. Herein lays the crux of the interaction of Officers, NCOs, and enlisted personnel. Careerism and routine erode this relation. The answer to this question is the burden of a "good officer." Our military is driven by social and political forces that are at odds with the discipline and ability to execute a mission, i.e. follow orders.

The ultimate reality is that we serve. Service before self—a common enough phrase, a buzzword, a rallying point but also a paradox.

A good friend once asked for bullet statements for my retirement. I told him I had nothing significant to give him. I had served, sometimes better than other times, I had my share of screw ups but I can honestly say I never did anything intentionally malicious.

Chapter Twelve:
Good Order and Discipline

The Open Door Policy

There are issues with an open door policy. Originally, it probably was a good idea, but like so many good ideas it has become co-opted by those with special and private interests. Special and private interests usually can be defined as those interests that go against good order and discipline.

I tell the story in *Anderson's Rules* about the time my second granddaughter Rachel came to our house for the first time when she was thirteen months old. I have always said my family has a defective gene, we collect rocks. When Pam and I bought the house I even put in a rock garden and convinced the kids it was where we grew rocks.

Anyway, Rachel and I would go out to the rock garden four or five times a day, that was "Paw Paw" time. She would cover her feet and shoes in the gravel and inevitably pick up a rock and move to place it in her mouth; I would go aaaannngh.

We repeated this process four or five times a day for seven days. On the eighth day, Rachel picked up a rock and stopped before putting it in her mouth and waited on me to go aaaannngh.

On the ninth day, she picked up a rock, covertly threw it away and acted as though she had put it in her mouth and was chewing it. That showed me that whether you are thirteen months, thirteen years, thirty-three or fifty-three, we are all still children that like to play and see how far we can push the envelope of rules and boundaries.

The same is true with troops and employees. They need guidance and rules even though no one likes them. When a Commander has an open door policy, he/she needs to be careful and use that policy correctly.

One unit I was with is a prime example of what I'm talking about. The Group Commander, a Colonel, had an open door policy that was nothing more than a way for subordinates to completely by-pass the Squadron Commander and Senior NCOs.

Once the junior NCOs realized they had a direct line to a senior officer, every time they did not agree with what the squadron leadership was doing, they would go complain to the Colonel.

In their minds they did not have to do their jobs. The Colonel would handle it for them. This is like when Dad says something and the kids go to Mom to get him to change. Pretty soon, Mom and Dad are fighting with each other and the kids are running the family.

The end result was on-going drama and turmoil and this was in a military unit.

Remember, whether you are thirteen months, thirteen years, thirty-three or fifty-three, we are all still children that like to play and see how far we can push the envelope of rules and boundaries.

Those in the military (or in civilian companies) that have their own agenda can subvert supervision to the point that the inmates are running the asylum. Senior commanders allow this to occur by participating in it.

Open door policies are okay, when they are used correctly. In fact, they are a check and balance for when a subordinate commander becomes abusive or is off track.

The first question a senior commander or senior NCO should ask when someone uses the open door policy is, "Have you discussed this with your supervisor?"

I can guarantee that most haven't and the session ends up being a "b***h" session and gossip visit. When a senior allows that to occur they undermine the authority of a junior supervisor, create a by-pass for the disgruntled and undermine good order and discipline. Major Mark A. Smith Sr., U.S. Army (ret) once said, "Senior officers who allow discussions about a brother officer, not present, are not honorable men."

I know that right now the tone of the presentation is pretty somber. But it is necessary to see how dark it is if we are going to appreciate the light. You have to understand that where we are as a country, as individuals is dynamic.

We all have the power and tools to change the circumstances we are in but we first have to change our attitudes, and we need to do this as it relates to rules.

Rules eliminate or reduce options and decisions. If we are in a state of confusion or stress, how much decision-making do we need to be doing any way?

Each of us is made up of a number of self-images or identities. We are white, black, Hispanic Asian, Native American—or whatever. We are tall, short—or whatever. We are well educated, not educated—or whatever. We are male, female—or whatever. We are Republican, Democrat—or whatever. We are victims, volunteers or victors.

Some of these identities are chosen for us; some we chose. And we can choose from a multitude of self-images and identities. I am a son, a brother, a husband, a father and a grandfather. I am a Texan. I am an American. I am a retired NCO. I am a retired Chief Master Sergeant, a Veteran, a safety professional, a human resource specialist, a double doctorate, and I am many other things.

The more complex the title, the more written rules to simplify the process it seems. I have all of the rules I will need to be successful in my roles. As an American, I have laws (which are rules), but rules are not always a lot of fun.

Awards and Decs

The awards and decorations program is a terrible two-sided sword that drips poison from the blade. The "gamers" put themselves in for everything while hard workers don't have the time or energy to; they are working.

Lazy supervisors fail to submit decorations for their people because they view it as a "pain in the butt" rather than a legitimate part of supervision. Why is it a pain? Most supervisors do a lousy job of documentation. Therefore they can't remember what happened six weeks or six months ago.

Awards and decorations should be used to acknowledge competence, hard work and "above average" activities. They are important to the troops; they should be important to supervisors.

I was at a Guard function one time and saw a Chief Master Sergeant with medals covering the entire left side of his Mess Dress. I had never seen so many medals in my career. I was talking to one of his troops who commented that the Chief had not put anyone else in for a medal in over two years; just himself.

Perception vs. Evidence

Perception should never trump evidence! Lazy management listens to the disgruntled, and forms opinions and then takes actions that are always detrimental to good order and discipline.

Listen to the complaint and investigate! For Pete's sake, how hard is that? If the complaint is valid then act on it, but don't allow yourself to be "gamed"; you will if you don't do your own due diligence.

When a senior supervisor allows that to occur they undermine the authority of a junior supervisor, create a by-pass for the disgruntled and undermine good order and discipline.

Thinking Out of the Box

I heard a story once about a Chinese General that laid siege to the town and the siege had lasted seven years. Neither the General nor the town could win a lasting victory or the upper hand. The General called for a meeting with the Mayor. He said, "I am willing to leave but I must be able to save face in front of my men."

Mayor – That is reasonable, how can I help?

General – Give me a tribute and I will quit the field immediately.

Mayor – Oh, great General what tribute do you wish? Gold? Jade? What?

General – One thousand pigeons.

Mayor – That is all? One thousand pigeons and you will leave?

General – One thousand pigeons.

The Mayor agreed and returned to the town. One thousand pigeons were captured and put in one thousand small cages. They were delivered to the General.

While the General's men were making a big production of packing up and breaking camp, a small work force tied oil soaked rags to the legs of each pigeon. At a signal from the General, all were lighted and the pigeons set free.

They immediately flew back to the town to their nests. The town burned down and the General marched through the walls in victory.[1]

Chapter Thirteen:
Personal Development

We Learn From Failure, Not Success

We do not learn from success—we celebrate it. We learn best from failure and embarrassment.

Also in *Anderson's Rule's*, I talk about one of the basic tenants of human adult learning is that we learn from making mistakes and avoiding making those same mistakes again. When we fail and fail miserably, it is in that failing we make decisions that determine our own futures. We didn't like failing, so we avoid failing again—by getting better at what we failed at.

When I was a child we used to play baseball in my neighborhood. Some of these kids were really good at baseball and were always picked first for the teams. Many of us were picked later or not at all. We were not that good at baseball.

The rule was simple—if you wanted to play, you had to learn to play better. Again, if you are willing to do what is necessary to be successful you will be successful.

Treasure your failures. By failing, you find out where and what you need to improve. If you get out there and practice pitching, catching, fielding and throwing, and show improvement, you'll get picked for the team. If you don't practice and improve, you don't get picked.

It is as simple as that and remains a basic premise of the real world. Even attempts such as affirmative action could not override this premise. Those being discriminated against should not be given opportunities to succeed in spite of their abilities.

Rather they should fight against established patterns of behavior by the majority of society—and win.

Later on, when presented with a level playing field, many individuals rose to the occasion and developed those skills necessary to keep that position and succeeded even further. And they did it on their own merit.

Unfortunately, we continue to try to make the world fair. We continue to try to eliminate failure. On the surface that does not sound too bad. I have failed and I hated it. It was embarrassing. It did not feel good. In reality the world is not fair and if you eliminate failure, you eliminate excellence.

The ONLY way to be truly successful is to get an opportunity. I have always said, "Just give me an opportunity to show you what I can do."

Many other folks said that and, unfortunately, they showed us what they can (or can't) do. Many failed to continue developing themselves, and they bastardized the process. They turned America into an "entitlement society" that believes society owed them something.

I believe that each individual is owed the opportunity to succeed but I do not believe every individual will or SHOULD be successful. The world does not work that way. Success is earned, not given.

Excellence is the correspondent of failure—you cannot have one without the other. The attempt to eliminate failure will only eliminate excellence and homogenize the gene pool. We would then gain the dubious distinction of being able to be just like everyone else.

I don't want to be like anyone else. While there are many characteristics in many people that I value and strive to make mine, I am a unique creation of the Almighty. His task for me is to excel at being me. Don't be afraid to try something new. I've heard it said, "Remember, an amateur built the ark. Professionals built the Titanic."

You are a work of art but the art is unfinished. Art like almost everything else worthwhile takes courage. More than anything else, it takes courage to try. It takes more courage to succeed.

Embrace Mistakes

It takes courage to go through the military, just as it takes courage to simply go through life. No one starts out knowing everything. No one starts out with good judgment. Someone said, "Good judgment comes from a lot of bad experiences!"

I am supposed to strive against odds and to succeed, not in spite of those odds, but because of them. We learn nothing from our successes, we are not supposed to. We are supposed to celebrate them.

We only learn through failure. Children learn by their successes. As we get older, we learn to avoid punishment, embarrassment and failure. I'm saying try your best not to screw up; but when you do, embrace the screw up and don't do it again.

It is important that leaders allow their folks to fail. You don't want to make a habit of it and you don't want them making the same mistakes over and over.

It is important that they figure out how and why they fail. If you constantly "rescue" you are "enabling" not helping them.

It is the failures and bad things that have happened in your life that have made you who you are. These are the things that have strengthened you and given you character.

This is particularly true of NCOs!

A Good NCO is Like a Whetstone

One of the most basic and primary jobs of a Sergeant is to be a whetstone. He is the standard by which the troops (and even Officers) should measure themselves by. A good NCO is like a fine whetstone.

It is always there, always ready and always gets the job done; but like the good stone, he should be appreciated and used correctly and maintained correctly.

Otherwise, the "edge" on a new troop or young officer will be inefficient. I have seen far too many good NCOs get tired of the games, the political correctness and politics. "Touchy feely" and "kinder and gentler" are not the characteristics of a good whetstone or good NCO. That would be like trying to sharpen a knife on a banana.

Living is Like Sharpening a Knife

"Do you know how to sharpen a knife?" You rub it against something that is harder than the knife. You must have the right angle. You must balance the number of strokes on each side of the blade, or the edge will not be even.

The same applies to us as people. Find something or someone that is "harder" than you are and try your best to incorporate those good qualities into yourself.

Get the right "angle." That angle will always be how you can serve someone else, not yourself. Find the "balance" by doing right things, the right way, every day.

Some people will come into your life and "sharpen" you by showing you how to live. Some people will come into your life and "sharpen" you by showing you how NOT to live; both can teach you, one is just more fun than the other.

Adults learn faster by trying to avoid pain and embarrassment than by any other method. As also previously stated, "We learn nothing from our successes; we are not supposed to. We are supposed to celebrate them."

We only learn from those things at which we fail, those things that cause pain and embarrassment. Children learn slowly by their successes. Older folks learn faster by learning how to avoid punishment, embarrassment and failure. Fortunately or unfortunately, it is the way of things.

I have often pondered the question, "What would you change in your life?" Like most folks, for years I contemplated what would I change if I could go back in time. What mistakes would I not make? What could I do to avoid hurting the people I have hurt? What disasters would I be able to avoid? Then I came to realize that all of the things I would like to have changed or avoided or should have prevented were part of what has made me who I am today.

Everything that has come into my life—every friend, every enemy, every opportunity, every failure, every accomplishment, every embarrassment, every goal achieved and every goal denied have all worked together to make me exactly who I am at this moment.

This is particularly true of those things that I would consider negative in my life. Again, I do not believe we learn from successes, we celebrate them. Some folks do not learn from their failures either, but I have tried. I think for the most part I have succeeded.

I have learned that everyone has the potential for making mistakes. I have learned that society is not the best determinate of my behavior—I am. I have learned that I could lie, cheat, steal, lust, betray friends and seek comfort from my enemies.

I have learned that integrity is only integrity as long as it is protected and defended. I have learned that fear can be a friend; it keeps you from being stupid. I have learned that courage is not the absence of fear; rather it is the controlling of that fear.

In the "old days," bad things happened to good people. People were expected and required to "get past" those bad things. Previous generations recognized that individual events were a poor standard by which to evaluate life. Invariably, people grew stronger for having combated the negative forces they encountered.

During the sixties, we began to realize that events and tragedies had a tremendous impact on human beings. Those impacts could last for days, months, years or in some cases, remain for a lifetime.

We discovered that the "combat fatigue" experienced by soldiers during World War II and previous conflicts was better named "Post Traumatic Stress."

My Dad, like many soldiers from World War II saw horrific things. He felt fear, he saw friends killed in front of his own eyes. He carried those images with him until the day he died; but he, like many other men and women who are placed in traumatic conditions, did his very best to "get past" those isolated and terrible events.

He decided that he would not let those terrible events define his life. Rather, he would use those terrible events to help refine his life. There was no way to stop the visions, but he learned to deal with them as dreams, horrible memories, but just that—memories.

The memory is a magical thing. A song, a scent or a sight can instantly transport a human mind through days, years or decades to a previous event. And while the human mind explores the reliving of that event, the event is almost real again. The operative phrase is "almost."

It is a condition of living that we humans will suffer. It is a condition of living that we humans will fail. It is a condition of living that terrible things will happen that can affect us for a long time.

It is also a condition of living that we humans will prevail. It is a condition of living that we humans will succeed. It is a condition of living that wonderful things will happen that can affect us for a long time.

Our job as humans is to determine where we will focus our attention and our intention. George Santayana said, "He who fails to remember the past is destined to repeat it."

He was correct, but I would add, "He who fails to remember the past and learn from it will repeat the past."

The definition of crazy is doing the same thing again and again and again and again the same way, and expecting it to turn out differently. Avoiding this trap requires experience and evaluation and a change in actions and thoughts that will allow for success.

This is where the analogy of knife sharpening comes in. The knife becomes sharper by rubbing it against something that is harder than it is, the correct way and the correct number of times on each side.

I have accomplished many things in my life that I am proud of, but there are things in my life that I am deeply ashamed of. It is that shame that keeps me from doing things I was able to justify in the past.

It is not so much that I enjoy living in the wonderful light I have found. More, it is that I never want to go back into the darkness of where I was.

If you read this and the message resonates with you and you are in that darkness, know that you have chosen that pit you are in and you can choose to climb out of it.

If you are reading this and you are someone I have wronged in the past, please accept my sincerest and most heartfelt apology. Please know there is not a day that goes by I don't think of the wrongs I did. That constant memory has molded my behavior and my life and by not doing that to anyone else, I am better. God bless all of you who have come into my life and have been a sharpening stone for me. Thank you.

PART FOUR: MILITARY TRADITIONS AND MORE

Chapter Fourteen:
Military Honors and Ceremonies

Some of you may have seen this ceremony, but did not understand it. Below explains the significance of the ceremony:

Missing Man Table and Honors Ceremony[1]

Moderator: As you entered the dining area, you may have noticed a table at the front, raised to call your attention to its purpose—it is reserved to honor our missing loved ones [or missing comrades in arms for veterans].

Set for six, the empty places represent Americans still [our men] missing from each of the five services—Army, Navy, Marine Corps, Air Force, Coast Guard—and civilians. This Honors Ceremony symbolizes that they are with us, here in spirit.

Some [here] in this room were very young when they were sent into combat; however, all Americans should never forget the brave men and women who answered our nation's call [to serve] and served the cause of freedom in a special way.

I would like to ask you to stand, and remain standing for a moment of silent prayer, as the Honor Guard places the five service covers and a civilian cap on each empty plate.

Honor Guard: (In silence or with dignified, quiet music as background, the Honor Guard moves into position around the table and simultaneously places the covers of the Army, Navy, Marine Corps, Air Force and Coast Guard, and a civilian hat, on the dinner plate at each table setting. The Honor Guard then departs.)

Moderator: Please be seated... I would like to explain the meaning of the items on this special table.

The table is round—to show our everlasting concern for our missing men.

The tablecloth is white—symbolizing the purity of their motives when answering the call to duty.

The single red rose, displayed in a vase, reminds us of the life of each of the missing, and the[ir] loved ones and friends of these Americans who keep the faith, awaiting answers.

The vase is tied with a red ribbon, symbol of our continued determination to account for our missing.

A slice of lemon on the bread plate is to remind us of the bitter fate of those captured and missing in a foreign land.

A pinch of salt symbolizes the tears endured by those missing and their families who seek answers.

The Bible represents the strength gained through faith to sustain those lost from our country, founded as one nation under God.

The glass is inverted—to symbolize their inability to share this evening's [morning's/day's] toast.

The chairs are empty—they are missing.

Let us now raise our water glasses in a toast to honor America's POW/MIAs and to the success of our efforts to account for them.

Table Set Up:

1. A small, round bistro table
2. White tablecloth
3. Single place setting, preferably all white
4. Wine glass—inverted
5. Salt shaker
6. Slice of lemon on bread plate with a pile of spilled salt
7. Small bud vase with a single stem red rose
8. RED ribbon tied around the vase
9. Candle—lit
10. Empty chair

"When we assumed the Soldier, we did not lay aside the Citizen."

—General George Washington, New York Legislature, 1775

History of the Challenge Coin[2]

During World War One, American volunteers from all parts of the country filled the newly formed flying squadrons. Some were wealthy scions attending colleges such as Yale and Harvard who quit in mid-term to join the war. In one squadron, a wealthy lieutenant ordered medallions struck in solid bronze and presented them to his unit.

One young pilot placed the medallion in a small leather pouch that he wore about his neck. Shortly after acquiring the medallions, the pilot's aircraft was severely damaged by ground fire. He was forced to land behind enemy lines and was immediately captured by a German patrol. In order to discourage his escape, the Germans took all of his personal identification except for the small leather pouch around his neck.

In the meantime, he was taken to a small French town near the front. Taking advantage of a bombardment that night, he escaped. However, he was without personal identification.

He succeeded in avoiding German patrols by donning civilian attire and reached the front lines. With great difficulty, he crossed no-man's land. Eventually, he stumbled onto a French outpost. Unfortunately, saboteurs had plagued the French in the sector.

They sometimes masqueraded as civilians and wore civilian clothes. Not recognizing the young pilot's American accent, the French thought him to be a saboteur and made ready to execute him.

He had no identification to prove his allegiance, but he did have his leather pouch containing the medallion. He showed the medallion to his would-be executioners and one of his French captors recognized the squadron insignia on the medallion.

They delayed his execution long enough for him to confirm his identity. Instead of shooting him they gave him a bottle of wine.

Back at his squadron, it became tradition to ensure that all members carried their medallion or coin at all times. This was accomplished through challenge in the following manner—a challenger would ask to see the medallion.

If the challenged could not produce a medallion, they were required to buy a drink of choice for the member who challenged them. If the challenged member produced a medallion, then the challenging member was required to pay for the drink.

This tradition continued on throughout the war and for many years after the war while surviving members of the squadron were still alive. We proudly continue this tradition today with the challenge coin.

———————————

"Coin Check" Rules[3]

1. A "Coin Check" consists of a challenge and response. A challenge is initiated by either holding your coin in the air or slamming it on a table or floor and yelling "Coin Check!"

2. Individual(s) challenged must respond by showing their Coin with their own unit's logo to the challenger within 10 seconds.

3. Anyone challenged who doesn't show their Coin must buy a round of drinks for all challenged, including the challenger.

4. Coin Checks are permitted anywhere and anytime.

5. If everyone being challenged produces their Coin, the challenger must buy a round of drinks for all challenged.

6. If you accidentally drop your Coin and it makes an audible sound on impact, then you "accidentally" initiated a Coin Check.

7. There are no exceptions to the rules. They apply to clothed or un-clothed (that means naked or not). One step and an arm's reach are allowed.

8. A Coin is a Coin. They are not belt buckles, key chains or necklaces. Coins worn in a holder around the neck are valid.

Always carry your coin as a reminder of your commitment and connection to something bigger in your daily life.

My Coin

When I learned that I was to become the Command Chief Master Sergeant for the 147th Fighter Wing at Ellington Field, I began to design my personal coin. At that point in time, becoming Command Chief was the high point of my military career.

I wanted the coin to do many things. I wanted to identify the salient points that had moved my career to this zenith. I wanted it to identify my unit and my position. I also wanted to honor my family. It took three months to finalize the design.

Because it is unique, I have received a lot of questions concerning the symbols on this coin. On the obverse, my position and wing are identified above the chevron for the Command Chief Master Sergeant. Below the chevron is the name of my base at that time, Ellington Field. Below that is my given name, my nickname and my status as a PhD.

On the reverse, across the top of the coin is the question "Can you shoot your own dog?" The meaning for this I described in the chapter on leadership, dealing with Ol' Yeller.

In the center is a blue feather. The significance of this comes from Richard Bach's book, *Illusions—The Adventures of a Reluctant Messiah*. This is probably the most significant book I have ever read and to date I have read it 59 times.

In *Illusions*, there is a description on how to "magnetize good things into your life." In the book, a blue feather was used as an illustration. Each time I have "magnetized" a blue feather, I have actually found one.

During a particularly lousy time in my life around 1988, I left my house for a five mile jog. As I always did, I drew a line in the sand and gravel of the road and started running. This day I decided I was in serious need of some "magic" and I went through the process described in *Illusions* for magnetizing.

As I ran past the finish line I noticed there was a feather— a blue feather lying on the line I had drawn. I went back and retrieved the feather. I had never seen one like it before. On one side, it was a beautiful deep blue; on the other side it was golden.

Three weeks later, I saw my first tropical blue Macaw. I realized the feather I found had come from such a bird. Now, I don't know what the odds are of a blue Macaw, flying over northwest Louisiana on that day, at that time and dropping a single blue feather and having it land exactly on that line; but, it impressed the hell out of me. So I put some magic on that coin and added a blue feather.

If you want to learn more about this magic, I recommend you read a special book called *Sacred Feathers—The Power of One Feather to Change Your Life*, by Maril Crabtree. It contains numerous stories of feather magic. I was fortunate to be able to tell my blue feather story in this book.

To the left of the feather is a glyph my son John designed when he first read *Lord of the Rings* by J.R.R. Tolkin. Below it are the initials SK, these are for John's daughters, my granddaughters, Sarah and Kayleigh. To the right of the feather is a bear's head; my daughter Shelley's childhood nickname was Sugar Bear. Below it are the initials RJS, these are for Shelley's children, my granddaughter, Rachel, and my grandsons, Josh and Seth.

Next is the statement "Everything and more." One of the best officers I ever served under was my dear friend, David A. Bond, Col, USAF (Ret). He has the Bond family motto, "Even the world is not enough" on his wall.

I thought that was really neat and set out to come up with the Anderson motto. It became — Everything and More! That is what I want out of life.

Finally the most unusual item on the coin is the word PAROMEBELART. Now if you ask my son, he'll tell you it is Latin for "Kill them all, let God sort them out." In reality, it is my name and my wife's name intertwined.

Pamela and Robert: PA   ME   LA
                    RO   BE   RT

The Blade of Honor Ceremony

The Blade of Honor Ceremony was a tradition practiced at the 917th Medical Squadron at Barksdale AFB, LA. The first ceremony was the presentation of an English Medieval Sword and certificate to my buddy Jim Singleton. The certificate read:

The Blade of Honor

No one is sure when the first sword was given as a reward, an acknowledgment or as sign of high respect. Probably, it was shortly after swords were invented in that period of ancient history.

Making a sword was and is an expensive, difficult and time-consuming process. The gift of a sword conveyed the highest honor and respect. It conveyed brotherhood and appreciation. It was not and is not a simple gesture.

A sword is forged in white hot heat, as a man is forged by the difficulties forced on him by circumstance or his own choices.

The blade must be tempered; hard enough to shear armor yet flexible enough not to break. The man must also be tempered to withstand difficulty and do hard things while remaining compassionate enough to help the weak and defend those who cannot defend themselves. Above all—neither blade nor man may ever break.

The blade must have a handle by which it can be gripped. The man must have standards by which he keeps in accord with God and duty.

The blade must have a sheath in which it can be carried and protected between battles. A man, a lucky man, has a spouse and family that is his place of repose between the battles of life and the turmoil of duty.

The sword must be polished and appointed appropriately to bestow honor upon the man to whom it is given.

The man receiving the sword must be polished and well-appointed to do honor to a blade forged in the fires of hell; to defend the gates of heaven—tempered with care to be used recklessly—sharpened against something harder than it is—in the hopes it will never be used.

This is the story of the Sword—and the story of the Man.

James J. Singleton, former ART, forever friend, able leader and brother-in-arms this blade comes to you—touched by each of us—as **you** have touched each of us. May it serve you as well as you have served us.

With undying appreciation and our highest respect, WE give to the man—**MSgt JAMES J. SINGLETON**—this sword; forever named—HONOR. From the Officers, NCOs and Enlisted Members of the 917th Medical Squadron Barksdale AFB, LA, Given this date, 7 May 2000 (By Bob Anderson).

Jim went on to retire as a Chief Master Sergeant at another base.

Chapter Fifteen:
Military Sayings and Humor

The AttaBoy Certificate[1]

This is to acknowledge

that _____ is

hereby awarded the Atta Boy Certificate for
outstanding performance during Operation

_____.

and is hereby
recognized and commended for his/her actions.

Note: You are reminded that 10,000 Atta Boys can be wiped out
by one "oh, s--t"!

"We are the untrained, doing the
impossible for the ungrateful."[2]

"We the willing, led by the unknowing, are doing the impossible
for the ungrateful. We have done so much, with so little, for so
long, we are now qualified to do anything, with nothing."[3]

—Konstantin Josef Jireček

How the Military Has Changed Over the Years...[4]

1945 - NCO's had a typewriter on their desks for doing daily reports.

1999 - Everyone has an Internet access computer, and they wonder why no work is getting done.

1945 - We painted pictures of girls on airplanes to remind us of home.

1999 - They put the real thing in the cockpit.

1945 - If you got drunk off duty your buddies would take you back to the barracks to sleep it off.

1999 - If you get drunk they slap you in rehab and ruin your career.

1945 - You were taught to aim at your enemy and shoot him.

1999 - You spray 500 bullets into the brush, don't hit anything, and retreat because you're out of ammo.

1945 - Canteens were made of steel, and you could heat coffee or hot chocolate in them.

1999 - Canteens are made of plastic, you can't heat anything in them, and they always taste like plastic.

1945 - Officers were professional soldiers first and they commanded respect.

1999 - Officers are politicians first and beg not to be given a wedgie.

1945 - They collected enemy intelligence and analyzed it.

1999 - They collect your pee and analyze it.

1945 - If you didn't act right, the Sergeant Major put you in the brig until you straightened up.

1999 - If you don't act right, they start a paper trail that follows you forever.

1945 - Medals were awarded to heroes who saved lives at the risk of their own.

1999 - Medals are awarded to people who work at headquarters.

1945 - You slept in barracks like a soldier.

1999 - You sleep in a dormitory like a college kid.

1945 - You ate in a mess hall, which was free, and you could have all the food you wanted.

1999 - You eat in a dining facility, every slice of bread or pat of butter costs, and you better not take too much.

1945 - We defeated powerful countries like Germany and Japan.

1999 - We come up short against Iraq and Yugoslavia.

1945 - If you wanted to relax, you went to the rec center, played pool, smoked and drank beer.

1999 - You go to the community center, and you can play pool.

1945 - If you wanted beer and conversation you went to the NCO or Officers' Club.

1999 - The beer will cost you $2.75, membership is forced, and someone is watching how much you drink.

1945 - The Exchange had bargains for soldiers who didn't make much money.

1999 - You can get better and cheaper merchandise at Wal-Mart.

1945 - We could recognize the enemy by their Nazi helmets.

1999 - We are wearing the Nazi helmets.

1945 - We called the enemy names like "Krauts" and "Japs" because we didn't like them.

1999 - We call the enemy the "opposing force" or "aggressor" because we don't want to offend them.

1945 - Victory was declared when the enemy was defeated and all his things were broken.

1999 - Victory is declared when the enemy says he is sorry.

1945 - A commander would put his butt on the line to protect his people.

1999 - A commander will put his people on the line to protect his butt.

1945 - Wars were planned and run by generals with lots of important victories.

1999 - Wars are planned by politicians with lots of equivocating.

1945 - We were fighting for freedom, and the country was committed to winning.

1999 - We don't know what we're fighting for, and the government is committed to social programs (used to be called 'socialism').

1945 - All you could think about was getting out and becoming a civilian again.

1999 - All you can think about is getting out and becoming a civilian again.

The NCO[5]

Submitted by SFC David Desselle, Army National Guard

A balloonist in a hot air balloon realized he was lost. He reduced altitude and spotted a man below. He descended a bit more and shouted, "Excuse me, can you help me? I promised a friend I would meet him an hour ago, but I don't know where I am."

The man below replied, "You're in a hot air balloon hovering approximately 30 feet above the ground. You're between 40 and 41 degrees north latitude and between 59 and 60 degrees west longitude."

"You must be an NCO," said the balloonist.

"I am," replied the NCO, "How did you know?"

"Well," answered the balloonist, "everything you told me is technically correct but I've no idea what to make of your information and the fact is I'm still lost. Frankly, you've not been much help at all. If anything, you've delayed my trip."

The NCO below responded, "You must be an Officer."

"I am," replied the balloonist, "but how did you know?"

"Well," said the NCO, "you don't know where you are or where you're going. You have risen to where you are due to a large quantity of hot air. You made a promise which you've no idea how to keep, and you expect people beneath you to solve your problems. The fact is you are in exactly the same position you were in before we met, but now, somehow it's my fault."

What NCOs Have Noticed About Officers[6]

- It's more important to look good than to be good.
- Non-matching furniture is a show-stopper. Untrained troops are not a show-stopper.
- A unit that has no money for new computers or spare parts will still manage to afford a big-screen TV for Power Point slide shows.
- A bad plan with good slides is better than a good plan with bad slides.
- Three sergeants thinking about an issue dealing with their MOS for four months and coming up with a detailed plan, is not as good as a colonel who knows nothing about their MOS or the problem thinking about it for 30 seconds.
- When you achieve high rank, the difference between what you know and what you feel fades away.
- The school officers go to aren't any better than the schools NCOs go to. But an NCO who goes to the ANCOC that deals with his MOS knows he's not necessarily smarter about his MOS; an Army officer who goes to an Air Force graduate school or a Joint College thinks he now knows more about the branch he's been away from for two years.

- A year's hard work by the troops can be destroyed because of some minor incident that happened to the Colonel when he was a lieutenant.
- Officers sit around thinking a lot. In a vacuum. This is not a good thing.
- Officers think they're businessmen. They think the principles used in business, like "corporate vision" and "TQM" can work in the Army. This is because officers spend a lot of time trying to sell things, usually grand ideas and catchy names.
- Officers believe that a plan won't succeed unless it has a good name, like "Operation Intrinsic Action." NCOs would rather give it something simple, like "Operation Beat Their ****** Heads In 5," and get on with it.
- Officers really do believe that a soldier is happier when he's busy, even if he's not doing what's important. NCOs know that nothing is so useless as doing well something which should not be done at all.
- There are a lot of officers out there who would have been better as NCOs, and a lot of NCOs who would have been better as officers.
- NCOs NEVER UNDER ANY CIRCUMSTANCES refer to other soldiers as "customers."
- Creating a twenty-minute slide show that makes the commander look good will get you the same medal as working you're a-- off for 12 months for the same commander.

Sixteen All-Time Biggest REAL Soldier Lies[7]

1. "I put it in distribution."
2. "Your pay will be straight at the end of the month."
3. "I know I left it right here on the top of my desk."
4. "Of course I can read a map."
5. "It's on valid requisition."
6. "No Sir, I don't smoke dope!"
7. "He's in the motor pool."
8. "I have to go back to the rear."

9. "I don't give a d@!& if the General hears about this!"
10. "I need this for the old man right away!"
11. "I was here until midnight last night working on this!"
12. "I read the after action report."
13. "Sorry I'm late, but the Colonel called me just as I was about to leave."
14. "Give me your number and I'll call you back."
15. "This is a courtesy inspection."
16. "We're here to help you."

PART FIVE: WAR STORIES

Chapter Sixteen:
War Stories

Author's Note:

The following story is from one of the best officers I ever served with. He is a most unusual man and exceptional friend. He is an honorable, Christian man, husband, father, grandfather and my pal. As you read this story you will find he did not retire. He knew he would never be able to retire. He served because he wanted to, without thought of compensation or benefits, he is my hero!

An Honor to Serve
By former USAFR Lt Col B.J. Garner, OD, BSC
Honorably Discharged

Photo submitted by B.J. Garner

"You are the man of the house now, son." These are some of the first words I remember my father saying to me. He was leaving home, bound for San Diego, California, to report for duty in the U.S. Navy. I was four years old. In my childlike way, I was prepared to do whatever was necessary to protect my mom, my younger brother, James, and my grandmother. My grandfather had passed away from a heart attack he suffered on my first birthday.

My dad's brother, Roy, was a naval aviator, flying combat missions, stationed aboard the USS Suwannee CVE 27 Scout Carrier. Dad was in the amphibious forces which stormed the beaches along with the Marines in the Central Pacific.

My Grandmother Garner told me she never knew when she awoke each morning if it might be the day she would receive a telegram telling her that either one or both of her sons had been killed in action.

Though my father and uncle returned home safely, the stress of those years caused Mom to plead with me and my three younger brothers not to join the military. Despite a strong desire to follow in the footsteps of my father and grandfathers who served their country in wartime, all sons honored our mother's request that she never see any of her sons in uniform.

When the Viet Nam conflict began, I was already married and working as a Registered Pharmacist. Married men were exempt from the Selective Service Draft at that time. Since Pharmacy was classified as a "Critical Civilian Profession," I was never "called up."

Eleven years later, I returned to college and received my Doctor of Optometry degree. The Viet Nam War was over and I had a wife and two elementary school daughters who needed me at home to provide for them.

During the next fifteen years, life was indeed full with family, church, and a busy optometry practice, but the desire to serve my country never left me. In the 1950's when I grew up, the difference between right and wrong was more black and white than it seems to be now. I felt that if you were right, you stood on it, and if somebody else had fought or died in my place, I was shirking my duty if I did not at least make the effort to do the same.

My wife, Laura, smiles as she recalls the day the Garners' lives dramatically changed. "On one of our drives home to Houston from east Texas, B.J. looked at me and asked, 'Is there something you always wanted to do but never did?'" She thought about it for a few minutes and said, "No, not really, how about you?"

In my frank, matter-of-fact way, I answered my wife with an emphatic, "Yes." I then began to tell her of my yearning to enter the military. In a time frame that only God could have designed, and just as I reached the milestone of having lived half a century, I was about to fulfill a lifelong dream.

In 1990, with one daughter a college graduate, and the other in her senior year of college, my mother died from cancer. Not long after that, postcards began appearing in my mailbox encouraging doctors to join the armed forces. It seemed that God was telling me that the time had come when He would give me the desires of my heart by serving my country in the military. A love of flying had been instilled in me by my uncle, the naval aviator, who had given me many informal lessons. The choice to enlist in the United States Air Force Reserve was easy.

But, when I walked into the recruiter's office, things became complicated. He looked me over and said, "I appreciate your interest, but I believe you're a little bit old." I was informed that, unfortunately, the age limit for enlistment was 42. After the recruiting officer learned that I was a doctor of optometry, however, his attitude changed. The recruiter said he did not know if it could be done, but he gave me a packet of materials to complete for an application. This was accomplished in short order and the packet forwarded to the Pentagon in Washington D.C. The following year included "background checks," age waivers, health exam, and also a determination of either my state of sanity or lack thereof.

I received a couple letters from Washington informing me that I "exceeded expectations." However, I was always told in a polite manner that I was not needed because the U.S. Air Force was following its age limitation regulation. It seemed that no one was willing to take a chance on a fifty-one year old junior officer.

I am a member of the South Belt-Ellington Chamber of Commerce. Since Ellington Field Joint Reserve Base is within the geographical area we serve, there are opportunities when our paths cross.

One day the Chamber of Commerce received notification that the Commanding General of the U.S. Air Force Reserve would be in Houston. We were invited to share in the official recognition banquet to welcome him to our city. We had two ordained ministers from local churches in our organization, but both had time conflicts and neither could attend. The Chamber Director then asked me to give the invocation before the meal.

Before I began the prayer, I read a passage from the Bible in Ephesians, Chapter 6, where St. Paul speaks about Christians putting on the full Armor of God. I reminded the audience that the symbol of the Air Force is the Shield. The shield is for protection. In the spirit of God and country, I prayed that the Almighty would guide the United States to "put on the shield of faith, whereby we shall be able to quench all the fiery darts of the wicked."

At the close of the prayer, we remained standing for the Pledge of Allegiance, the National Anthem and the instrumental rendition of the Air Force Hymn, "Wild Blue Yonder."

After the banquet, the General approached me to thank me for my prayer and tribute to the Air Force Reserve. He said that such a welcome is unusual from the civilian community. He asked me if I had served in the military. I told him no, however, I did have a desire to serve and had already completed the application packet to join the Air Force Reserve. To my dismay, there seemed to be no interest in me because of my being almost fifty-two years of age. He said he would see what he could do.

I found out later that the following Monday morning he dropped my packet on the desk of the Surgeon General of the Air Force Reserve and said, "I want this man. Take care of it." Within a week I received a telephone call from the Pentagon advising me that they were reviewing my application. They made no commitment, however. A few weeks later, a letter arrived at my home from the Pentagon. To my surprise, it was addressed to... "Captain Billy J. Garner, U.S. Air Force Reserve."

Skeptics might call everything that had transpired coincidental. However, I could not disagree more because:

- If the commanding General had not attended an official function at Ellington field,
- If I had not been a member of the Board of Directors for South Belt-Ellington Chamber of Commerce,
- If I had not been asked to give the invocation at the banquet,

- If I had not completed my packet and already sent it to Washington, D.C.,
- If it had not been God's timing, **I WOULD NOT HAVE GOTTEN INTO THE U.S. AIR FORCE.**

In 1991 I raised my hand and went into the military. It was something I had always wanted to do, yet I had stayed true to my mother's wishes.

Officer Training School at Lackland Air Force Base in San Antonio is a strenuous ordeal. Most men and women range in age from early to mid-twenties. At 52, I was ten years past any physical standards applicable to Air Force Recruits, so before leaving Houston I worked out with a young man from the Marine Reserve Officer Training Corps (ROTC). He ran with me and paced me so that I would be in top physical condition when I reported for duty. When I returned from officer training, I was in the best shape since I was 18 and played high school football.

Upon completion of Officer Training School in 1992, I realized a transformation had taken place. When I began OTS I went in as a doctor who had just joined the Air Force. When I came out, I was an Air Force Captain who was a doctor by profession. My duty then was to provide eye care to the pilots and support personnel of the Air Force.

My new orders were to report to Barksdale Air Force Base in Bossier City, Louisiana (near Shreveport) for monthly Reserve drills. During my first day of duty, I was introduced to the Air Force through an orientation to new inductees. The person in charge of the festivities was a fireball sergeant who was gung ho about the military.

I related to him immediately because our ideas and values were so similar. I found that interesting because I was just learning how to salute and he was already a seasoned non-commissioned officer. I listened intently to him as he reminded us of our duties and responsibilities as service members who had taken a solemn oath to "preserve, protect, and defend the Constitution of the United States."

He also told us what a privilege it was to wear the uniform of our country. I instantly admired this man. With Time-in-Grade he would be known as Command Chief Master Sergeant Robert M. Anderson.

Our camaraderie, based on friendship and respect, has grown stronger through the decades. A wise man once said, "A person should consider himself truly blessed if he has as many as five true friends in his lifetime." I have been so blessed because Bob Anderson is indeed my best friend.

While at Barksdale, my main duty was working with pilots. A person has to be totally free of visual impairments to be a pilot, but after those pilots are trained, they don't stop aging, and some begin to need visual care. Since the U.S. government had spent lots of money training those pilots, the question arose: Was there a possibility they could wear contact lenses in flight?

To answer that question, I was one of a few optometrists selected for a competitive program to determine if soft contacts could safely be worn by pilots. This involved a modified program of learning to fly. While I was not a fighter pilot, I did fighter pilot training. I did everything in an aircraft except take-off and land. In simulators I performed take-offs, landings, and combat maneuvers, and I memorized the entire cockpit so I didn't touch the wrong thing when I got in the real aircraft.

My training took me to nearby Ellington Field in Houston, Kelly Air Force Base in San Antonio, and as far away as Kingsley Field in Klamath Falls, Oregon. In Oregon, I participated in the F-16 Flight Surgeon Training Course called "Top Eye." At 54, I was twice the age of some of the participants who fondly gave me the handle of "Pop."

When I won the competition, which I attribute to my love of flying and previous training from my uncle, my handle quickly changed to "Pop Eye." It has stuck throughout my career. I'm not a flight surgeon, but I fall into a unique category of aerospace optometrist that was born during that time and still exists.

When I returned to Barksdale AFB, I began training as a B-52 co-pilot. I flew bomb runs with the group. It's a different kind of atmosphere. They fly into a situation where the crew realizes they may not return. It could be a one-way trip. In another of many unusual aspects of my military career, I realized that I was the only one of the flight crew who was older than the aircraft itself. But the engines of the B-52 have been modernized. They are faster and more fuel-efficient than they were in the 1960s, and we even had a microwave oven we used for long distance missions.

One of those missions was to Ramstein, Germany, in 1998, where I served with other reservists on a medical team treating survivors of the embassy bombings in Tanzania and Kenya. Many that were in the immediate area of the bombings were killed, but others were severely wounded by secondary blasts. We were treating Kenyans who were uneasy around the doctors until the reservists, many of whom were African-American, arrived, and they relaxed then. This was the only time that God allowed me to see the devastation of war that had so worried my mother. It was an experience that gave me a richer appreciation for the sacrifices of the military to maintain freedom around the world.

I had often been asked by my commander to give a special message during chapel for Christmas, Easter, or when out in the field. I realized that this was possibly the only time some of the airmen might attend a church service. I love to choose stories from military history that show how God has brought victory despite seemingly impossible odds.

One of my favorites is about Anna Warner, writer of the hymn, "Jesus Loves Me." Anna and her sister Susan held Bible study classes for the cadets across the Hudson River at the United States Military Academy at West Point from 1875 to 1915. These young men were taught the simple, yet profound, song and when they went off to World War I, it served them well. Those who fought in the Battle of the Meuse-Argonne in 1918 sang it as they marched to victory even though many of their fellow soldiers were falling beside them. About one in every ten soldiers died or was wounded during the onslaught. Later the American commanders were asked why they did not retreat. They gave as their inspiration the second verse of "Jesus Loves Me." It says: "Jesus loves me, He who died, Heaven's gates to open wide. If I love Him when I die, He will take me home on high."

That song was not written for children. It was written for men—men in battle—so they would remember that under every circumstance, "Jesus loves me this I know for the Bible tells me so." In honor of their military contribution, Anna and Susan Warner were the first women ever buried at West Point Military Cemetery.

From my point of view, it is so important that if you are going into the military and you know you might be in harm's way, you need to get right with the Lord first. It gives you the courage that you might not have otherwise because your future is already settled. We don't have to worry about giving our life for God; we have a God who has already given His life for us.

During my military career, I completed both Squadron Officer School and Air Command and Staff College, which is similar to graduate school, and moved up in the ranks to Lieutenant Colonel. Throughout my service in the military, I have maintained a private optometry practice.

My wife Laura and I are a team in our marriage, our optometry practice, and in my military involvement. Laura's support has been incredible, but she believes her support has been directly related to my efforts to involve her.

"He bent over backwards to enable me to be involved in what he did," Laura says. "That meant a great deal to me because I felt that I was participating. It made it so worthwhile to me and much more interesting and enjoyable. He worked hard to introduce me to his friends and be involved in whatever he did; otherwise, I might have had a feeling of resentment."

In 2004 I received an Honorable Discharge from the Air Force Reserve and participated in an exit ceremony. At the close of each drill, we have Commander's Call before dismissal. On my last day in uniform, our Medical Group Commander and all other Lieutenant Colonels had quietly left the building. I was the highest ranking officer in the assembly room. The First Sergeant called the room to attention and looked at me, indicating that I was in charge.

During all my years in the military, no one had ever called the room to attention for me. I was thrilled! It was a totally unexpected gift from the senior members of the officer corps. I strode up to the front of the room with my fellow Reservists at attention. I gave them a short speech reciting as much of the orientation speech that I could remember which Command Chief Master Sergeant Bob Anderson had given over a decade ago.

I also added some personal thoughts about my association with all those outstanding brothers and sisters in uniform. I then said, "That is all." The First Sergeant again called the room to attention. I, too, came to attention and gave them my best salute, performed an about face and walked out of the building.

As I left, I had three thoughts. Because of God's Grace:

- My Work Is Done
- I Have Fulfilled My Dream
- I Have Served My Country.

Author's Note: B.J. was a remarkable officer who got "it." What is "it?" I'm like the Supreme Court Justice who was asked to define pornography. He said, "I can't describe it but I know it when I see it." He is a husband, father, grandfather, was an excellent officer and is one heck of a friend. He is also my personal role model of a fine Christian man. That seems to give him peace and pleasure. It was an honor to serve with him.

*****

The Sarge
By former USAF Buck Sergeant Cary Hall
Honorably Discharged

Photos submitted by Cary Hall

In 1970, after completing my tour of duty in Vietnam as a dog handler with the 483rd SPS K9 unit, I was assigned a new duty station at Andrews Air Force Base in Washington D.C. I wasn't particularly happy about the assignment, since I had requested on my dream sheet to be assigned to Kadena Air Base in Okinawa or to Clark Air Base in the Philippines.

I had gone TDY to Kadena to pick up my second dog, Robon, while deployed in Vietnam, and had become quite enamored with the hospitality and the other opportunities Okinawa presented to a young G.I. Uncle Sam, however, had a different idea and, after a month and a half of accumulated leave, I reported to Andrews Air Force Base as a salty young buck sergeant (E-4).

Upon my arrival, I was not assigned to a K9 unit but to a standard security police detail, charged with the protection of Air Force 1 and the National Emergency Airborne Command Post. While it sounds prestigious, I thought the duty sucked.

After seeing action in the Nam for one year repelling sappers and the Viet Cong on a base that got hit eleven times, humping an airplane with an M16 was not a very glamorous duty. There was a 43-dog kennel at Andrews and a full-blown K9 unit, but there was no vacancy when I arrived.

As fate would have it, I applied for a job at the NCO club as a bouncer/bartender. The night manager turned out to be Master Sergeant Cunningham, the kennel master for the 1002nd SPS K9 unit which provided security and support to Andrews Air Force Base and to its mission as the home of Air Force 1 and the National Emergency Airborne Command Post.

After working with Master Sergeant Cunningham for a number of months, he befriended me and created an opportunity for me to join the K9 unit.

This was the beginning of one of the most important relationships in my young life. Master Sergeant Cunningham stood about 6' 3" and was from South Carolina (which wasn't hard to tell after he opened his mouth and directed you to do something).

The Master Sergeant sported spit-shined boots, an immaculate uniform and had a perfect flat-top haircut you could have landed an F-4 Phantom jet on. Master Sergeant Cunningham wasn't someone to be trifled with either. He commanded respect and was a strict disciplinarian with his troops.

It also turned out that he was a mentor to young enlisted men completing their initial four-year tour in the air force. If you proved yourself to the Master Sergeant, acted with integrity and were honest if you screwed up, the Master Sergeant would back you to the hilt. Little did I know, I soon would be needing Master Sergeant Cunningham's help.

After returning from Vietnam, a letter was sent by my former Master Sergeant at Cam Ranh Bay to the Chief Master Sergeant of our security police squadron at Andrews Air Force Base.

The letter stated that I had left Vietnam owing a significant amount of money to my previous squadron. This was an outright lie as I had no debt. However, it was the word of a buck sergeant against the word of a senior enlisted man, and the Chief Master Sergeant at Andrews did not believe I was telling the truth.

He proceeded to threaten me with a court martial and an Article 15 if I refused to pay.

I consulted Master Sergeant Cunningham, who laid out a course of action, sending a letter to a former captain I had served under at Cam Ranh Bay. The captain looked into the matter and found out it was a scam being run by the sergeant on many of his departing troopers.

Master Sergeant Cunningham took me to our security police headquarters, presented the facts to the Chief Master Sergeant and took great pleasure in watching him eat a large helping of humble pie. This time I was in the right, but I would soon be in a situation where the circumstances would be quite different.

While serving at Andrews, I lived off base. One afternoon, I was late for a canine demonstration that our squadron was putting on for a group of dignitaries. To make matters worse, my dog Hugo, a 103-pound Belgian Shepherd, was the star of the show.

While speeding around Perimeter Road on my way to the kennel, a very angry Lieutenant Colonel pulled up next to my Ford Maverick, screaming and yelling. He then forced me off the road where he promptly chewed my ass, took my ID and advised me that I would be hearing from him. Not good, especially considering I had a line number for E-5 staff sergeant hanging in the balance.

Upon arriving at the kennel, Master Sergeant Cunningham asked me why I was late. I gave him the quick version. He said that we'd talk after the demonstration. Once we finished our show, I sat down and leveled with the Sarge, advising him that yes I was speeding and that I had screwed up.

As it turned out, Master Sergeant Cunningham was a personal friend of the Colonel who was in charge of the security police squadron stationed at Andrews. So, when the Lieutenant Colonel advised the Colonel of my grave infractions and lack of discipline, it didn't matter because Master Sergeant Cunningham and I had already made an appearance in front of the Colonel who advised me not to let it happen again and ended the discussion.

The lesson I took away from this incident was that as long as you were straight with the Sarge, he would take care of his troopers.

Master Sergeant Cunningham saw us as an elite unit with the unique responsibility at Andrews of providing protection for the President and the many arriving foreign dignitaries who came through Andrews Air Force base.

The job was serious business, and as long as you treated it that way and lived up to your responsibilities, you could count on Master Sergeant Cunningham to be in your corner if you needed him.

Master Sergeant Cunningham played a unique role in my life. It was his mentoring which led me to become involved in the United States Police K9 Association where I traveled to different cities competing in regional and national competition with my dog against civilian and other military working dog units.

In fact, Hugo and I did very well, placing 13th overall in national competition, the highest ranking ever by an Air Force dog team.

The Sarge was a man I grew to admire during my time at Andrews. Not all career or lifer senior enlisted men were of the caliber of Master Sergeant Cunningham.

Many were venial, vindictive and petty men who used their rank and privilege to make life miserable for lower ranking enlisted men who had no desire to remain in the military past their original enlistment.

Master Sergeant Cunningham, on the other hand, was the exception to the rule.

As a result of his example, mentoring and tutelage, I was highly recruited by civilian police departments in the Washington D.C. area and went on to become a police officer with Prince George's County police department in PG County, Maryland.

I always will remember returning to the base in my PG County police car and rolling up to the kennel only to have Master Sergeant Cunningham come out of the office, greet me with a "Hello Sergeant," a big smile and a hand shake and tell me how proud he was of my accomplishments.

While at Andrews, Master Sergeant Cunningham saw that I was awarded the Air Force Commendation medal and the Air Force Good Conduct medal for my service in Vietnam and for the conclusion of my tour at Andrews.

He was a remarkable man who I will remember forever for the leadership he exhibited and for the decency he showed me.

However, this story wouldn't be complete without a post script. If you believe in what goes around comes around, you're going to love this.

While working as a police officer in Prince George's county, I was assigned a morning detail to check out-of-state registrations in a particular housing complex located close to Andrews Air Force Base.

You see, military personnel would game the system and register their cars in their home state rather than in Maryland since Maryland's costs were significantly higher than most other states. For this reason, we would periodically cordon off certain housing areas, setting up road blocks in order to check every car against the driver's id which listed the home address.

Low and behold, at 7:00 a.m. in the morning, up drives the Lieutenant Colonel who ran me off the road at Andrews and who had threatened me with an Article 15 for speeding.

And, as it would turn out, the good Lieutenant Colonel was breaking the law in the state of Maryland.

I guess you could call it poetic justice as I walked up to his car with my sunglasses and 8-point police hat fitted snugly on my head. "License and Registration, Lieutenant Colonel," I said.

The first words out of his mouth were, "I wasn't speeding." My response, "I didn't say you were. License and Registration, please."

After he presented me with the appropriate documentation, I advised the Lieutenant Colonel that his address didn't match his registration and license plates.

Upon hearing this news, the Lieutenant Colonel became so belligerent that I removed him from his automobile; hand cuffed him, placed him under arrest, put him in the back of my patrol car and called a tow truck to impound his automobile.

On the way to the station, the Lieutenant Colonel recognized who I was and proceeded to become more agitated. I advised the Lieutenant Colonel, "You are just another civilian and have no rank out here. Keep your mouth shut until we get to the station or you'll have the privilege of riding in the trunk the rest of the way."

The Lieutenant Colonel was booked, put in a holding cell and spent the day waiting for his bond to be posted and released.

I don't think there was a story Master Sergeant Cunningham enjoyed more than when I presented him with the arresting paperwork for our favorite Lieutenant Colonel and proceeded to relay the tale.

Master Sergeant Cunningham's closing comment was, "I never liked that son of a bitch anyway and still don't. Good job, Sergeant."

*****

Semper Fi

By Frank Desselle, MSgt, USMC (Ret)

I owe a lot if not all of my success to the leadership traits and principles that I was taught to live by daily for more than 20 years as a U. S. Marine. I know that the standards that I live by today also are a direct reflection of the Core Values instilled in all Marines.

The courage to serve as a Marine honorably started in 1976 when being part of any branch of the Military was not the highest thing on most young men's to do list. The courage to prepare young men to be tactically and technically proficient in their MOS and war fighting skills to protect themselves and fellow Marines and to be victorious at whatever they pursue in life.

The courage after hurricane Katrina hit the gulf coast to move my family to Tennessee not having a home or a job to go to but knowing that I would succeed. The courage to Honor God, Country, Corps and Family and adhere to moral principles and maintain integrity.

These are the reasons I served as a U.S. Marine and have learned to always be thankful and appreciative for what I have or don't have. I can see better now that I am in the private sector that I am called upon for my opinion on the direction someone might take because of my military experience and decision making skills.

My commitment or obligation is to do my very best at whatever I pursue personally, professionally or spiritually is a value that all marines and former marines live by. We cannot always control the result or outcome of something or someone but we can do our very best to influence that end result. Our Core values, of course are Courage, Honor and Commitment.

Semper Fidelis, of course is our motto meaning always faithful. God bless and good night.

*****

Draft Card Burner!
By Paul Gregg, SMSgt, USAF (Ret)

Photo submitted by Paul Gregg

Imagine my surprise when my mail arrived on Okinawa back in my active duty U. S. Air Force days and I opened a letter from my parents and it contained my draft card. Did it mean I could be drafted into the military when I already had a couple years of active duty behind me?

I graduated from Greenwood High School in Greenwood, Indiana in 1965, when the war in Vietnam was heating up. We had to register for the draft and I remember there were different draft designations. My card showed "1-A" which meant I was eligible for draft into any of the military components that might need me.

Having been on active duty long enough to be a "buck sergeant" with three stripes, I was wondering what to do with my draft card. I joined the Air Force in October of 1965 and received my draft card around 1968.

The "Stars and Stripes" newspaper was printed and distributed to military bases all over the world. Also, in that era, draft card burning was public news in

America. Draft dodgers and those opposed to the U. S. military involvement in Vietnam were enjoying their fifteen minutes of fame when they would get media exposure burning their draft cards, or burning the U. S. flag, usually by group or mob gatherings.

I contacted the Kadena Air Base office of the "Stars and Stripes" and told them I thought it would be a good idea to have them take a picture of an active duty airman burning his draft card not in a show of defiance, but showing the draft card came too late and the draftee was already in the Air Force.

They took my picture and interviewed me and my story was in a subsequent issue of their newspaper. If I have a copy of the story, it is buried somewhere in a box of my memories from those active duty days; but I do have copies of the original picture and cannot help but smile as I look at myself holding my Zippo lighter, flame almost under the card.

I didn't really burn the card, and truly wish I could find it in my archives. Maybe someday I will find it and the story that gave me my fifteen minutes of fame.

*****

> May we never forget the sacrifices made when a country asks ordinary men and women to do extraordinary things in its name.
>
> **—Author Unknown**

Our Privilege of Serving in the US ARMY

By former US Army Corporal Gary L. Jones
Honorably Discharged

**On the left is John L. Jones
and on the right is Gary L. Jones.**
Photo submitted by Bobbie Jones

My brother John Jones and I volunteered to serve in the Army during the Korean War. Being twin brothers, it was with honor and deep appreciation that we were able to serve our Great Country in Japan together in the First Calvary Division.

Johnny went to Vietnam twice to fight in the war. As to our military character, we both maintained a strong commitment in discipline and perseverance. We never regret the discipline and correction that made us good and faithful soldiers.

The military discipline enabled us to become better citizens of the United States of America. Also, it strengthened us to become better parents to our own families. Our call to the ministry of the Gospel of Jesus Christ has been more effective because of our experiences in the military.

Johnny served twenty years in the Army and never regrets one day of giving his time in the Military. He retired as a First Sergeant.

We had seven brothers and one sister that served in the military from the Jones family. All received an honorable discharge.

Finally, we give thanks to God for His Grace and strength in serving in the Army. It was a special privilege and humble delight to be a part of the military service.

We will always hold high the men and women who are serving in the different military. May God bless them and protect their family while they serve our country.

Closing, when we think of the military we become very emotional with many feelings that still flow from our hearts. We give God all the glory and praise for being a part of the USA Military.

Respectfully submitted with Honor and a Salute,
Rev. Gary L. Jones

*****

September 11th—Two Years Later

By Shelley Anderson-Moore (The author's daughter)
(article printed in *Army Times* in 2003)

Many people ask me what is like for me since my husband was in the Pentagon when those cowardly terrorists struck our wonderful country. It was the same for me as for all Americans—time stood still as the hours passed until I heard his voice. I am lucky though—so lucky—I heard his voice again and still have him. My children still have their father. He lost friends—dear friends and the entire country lost precious things that day. Even those who did not lose a loved one felt like they did because that is how American's feel.

We grieved and we are still grieving and as I write this I hope we will always grieve. I hope this because to grieve is to remember and September 11, 2001, should never be forgotten. Our fellow Americans we lost that day should never be forgotten.

In remembering those terrible feelings of that day we show respect for the lives lost and we show respect for our emergency workers who keep us safe every day and for our many soldiers still away from home trying to keep us safe. I am tired of listening to people say we shouldn't be there—enough! Nobody likes war—especially our soldiers. They are away from their families, their aging parents, their children, and their pregnant wives. Yes, it is our responsibility as the strongest NATION in the world to be there and finish what was started. How can we forget 9/11 when our military men and women are still fighting? We simply cannot.

I send this in hopes that it does not sadden you, but it reminds you to love our country and support our precious military and emergency workers and our President.

God Bless America,
Shelley

*****

Lessons for a "Butter Bar"

By former Lieutenant and later Captain Gregg Deane
Honorably Discharged

I was a "Rotsee" jock. That's 1970's talk for a Reserve Officers Training Corps (ROTC) cadet. I wanted to be a pilot in the worst way. What better way to go to college, get a degree, and have the stepping stone to being a pilot. There was no desire to be a fighter pilot; I wanted to be a tanker or cargo pilot. What more did I have to know to be an Air Force officer? Just fill the tanks and let's go on a mission.

At least, that's what I thought; more about that later.

Between my sophomore and junior years in college, I developed a friendly relationship with a Staff Sergeant in our ROTC unit. For some reason, we just jelled together. I sought his advice and absorbed it like a sponge. Looking back, I believe that God put us together for a reason; that reason was to make me a more compassionate and effective leader.

145

One day, the Staff Sergeant told me that what we plan for ourselves might not happen. He said that I might have to supervise people.

"Who me? Nah, I was gonna cut holes in the sky."

But he was insistent. He told me to listen carefully to my NCO's. He said that a big problem with new commissioned officers was that they thought they knew everything. They were in charge. He said he didn't want that to happen to me.

He said to seek out the advice from your senior NCO's. Let them do what they do best. Provide assistance when it was requested. Be a good officer. Be successful.

As it turned out, I didn't make it through pilot training; seems like I had a tendency to land expensive airplanes very hard. As it turned out, I had a problem with depth perception. I guess it is important to know how far your plane is from the ground.

So, after a while with the Manned Personnel Center at Randolph AFB, I selected Security Police as my career field. I had a degree in political science with a minor in criminal justice. It was a natural fit.

I got my orders and was stationed at a Strategic Air Command (SAC) base in Arkansas. It was that or Minot, North Dakota. I wanted to be warm.

I arrived at the Air Base around midnight. Two days later, I was put in charge of B Flight, 97th Security Police Squadron. I didn't even have a complete uniform. I was the Shift Supervisor for 30 Law Enforcement and Security personnel. They in full uniforms, me in fatigues with a plastic nameplate.

I remembered what the Staff Sergeant told me. I took it to heart. I called my two senior NCO's of B Flight over to the side. Both of them looked at me like I was from Mars with my funky incomplete uniform.

As it turned out, one had 18 years in Security Police. He was a Technical Sergeant (E-7). The other had 15 years in Security Police and he was a Master Sergeant (E-8).

I proceeded to tell them that they had started in Security Police when I was in elementary school. I had no training in Security Police. I asked for them to train me. I wanted them to run their flights as they saw fit and if they needed my help or rank, all they needed to do was ask. If they would train me, I would listen. I would help.

Both said that the working relationship I described was good with them and that we'd get along fine.

Three days later, the SAC Operational Readiness Inspection (ORI) happened at our base. I was so new at my job I didn't even know what an ORI was. With their help, I managed to avoid the inspectors.

My flights did well, but the squadron failed. The inspection report said I did a great job. Lesson learned.

I kept that philosophy throughout my stint as a Security Police officer. I was real successful and had respect from the troops. My flight was singled out as the best flight when our Squadron won Best Security Police Squadron in the USAF in 1978.

Unfortunately for me, I was medically discharged from the Air Force later that year. I did go out on a high, albeit unsatisfied, note.

All because I listened to what my NCO's told me. All because a Staff Sergeant in ROTC saw something in me he liked and whispered in my ear.

*****

The Citizen Soldier[1]

Charlton Heston, a former Master Sergeant and acclaimed actor once said, "This country began on the shoulders of a citizen that took up arms to defend his country. From the first shot fired, the citizen soldier has been the backbone of this country's defense. While the regular military stands post all of the time; that force has NEVER been capable of protecting this country by itself, NOR SHOULD IT."

"This country is made of individuals. It is the duty of each to protect our families, our friends, our country, our national interests and our flag." God Bless.

—Charlton Heston

*****

Coming Home[2]

A story is told about a soldier who was finally coming home after having fought in Vietnam. He called his parents from San Francisco. "Mom and Dad, I'm coming home, but I've got a favor to ask. I have a friend I'd like to bring with me."

"Sure," they replied, "we'd love to meet him."

"There's something you should know," the son continued. "He was hurt pretty badly in the fighting. He stepped on a land mine and lost an arm and a leg. He has nowhere else to go, and I want him to come live with us."

"I'm sorry to hear that, son. Maybe we can help him find somewhere to live."

"No, Mom and Dad, I want him to live with us."

"Son," said the father, "you don't know what you're asking. Someone with such a handicap would be a terrible burden on us. We have our own lives to live, and we can't let something like this interfere with our lives. I think you should just come home and forget about this guy. He'll find a way to live on his own."

At that point, the son hung up the phone. The parents heard nothing more from him.

A few days later, however, they received a call from the San Francisco police. Their son had died after falling from a building, they were told. The police believed it was suicide. The grief-stricken parents flew to San Francisco and were taken to the city morgue to identify the body of their son.

They recognized him, but to their horror they also discovered something they didn't know, their son had only one arm and one leg.

*****

The Baker's Dirty Dozen

By former Army Warrant Officer Candidate Randall Hall
Honorably Discharged

About a thousand years ago, there was a time known as the "Vietnam era." After many tests and a long application process, I was accepted into the Army Warrant Officer Training Program for helicopter pilots.

As luck would have it, my career as a chopper pilot, "never got off the ground"!

One of the earliest and memorable episodes of that adventure was me and twenty guys lined up in our "all-togethers" presenting the "full Monty" while a nurse told us to turn our head and cough; I am not sure who got the most out of that, the guys or the nurses.

The next indignity was when she told us to bend over and grab our ankles. Once we finished the physicals, a Greyhound bus loaded with "fresh meat" headed to the "grinder" known as Ft. Polk, LA.

Upon our arrival, we immediately realized it was not the vacation spot we were led to believe. The drill instructors (DIs) were loud and in a hurry to get us to our rooms or room; "kinder and gentler"—not!

The good news—haircuts were free; the bad news—no matter what we asked for we all got the same haircut. The good news—we could get any color of army duds; the bad news—as long as they were O.D. (olive drab) green.

Then we had to mail our civvies (civilian clothes) home along with our brains.

Our first drill instructor was a huge bald headed guy that everyone hated, including (apparently) the prostitute in Leesville that shot him three times in the stomach. He lived but we were happy because we got a new DI that we actually liked.

Our new DI was Cajun and he always said, "How Bout that Shit!!" That was in the days before "Shit Happens."

Early one morning after our usual five minute breakfast, it was time to hit the road running. After about a quarter mile, one of the guys lagging behind gave up his breakfast. The DI made him pick it up and put it in his pocket.

I knew at that point that I was not being led by normal folks and I was not in Ar-Kansas anymore!

Little did I know I was already at the high point of my Army career! After a few weeks of stomach problems I finally realized it was not the food, I figured out I had a problem that Maalox from the infirmary alone, could not fix.

If the DIs could not see a problem, they thought you were faking it. So every day I was forced to pack up ALL of my gear and check it into supply to go the infirmary—just to get one bottle of Maalox. Then I had to check ALL of my gear back out of supply and set it back up for inspection.

After a few more weeks I finally got an appointment to see the Doctor. He believed my symptoms enough to at least call for an x-ray; they found an ulcer. Next stop for me was the U.S. Army Medical Hold Unit. There were thirteen of us assigned to the Hold Unit.

There's an old saying about if you are soldier in a foxhole being bombed you believed in God. I submit if you were in a medical hold unit at that time in history you also believed in God.

I remember some of the guys in this story by their first name, some by their last, but the one thing I do remember is they were a crazy bunch.

Of course, they were all drafted and I had volunteered. They thought I was crazy!

In 1969, the Hospital at Ft. Polk looked like a group of wooden barracks stuck end to end. They had been built during World War II like every other building there. We were told that was why we had to have a Fire Watch posted each night, because all of the barracks could burn up in 3 minutes.

It was a Court Martial offense if you fell asleep.

On the day that I had my x-rays done, I told the Doctor what I had to go through to get one bottle of Maalox and the fact it was not working. He gave me a prescription for Valium. I must say that was a great way to float through the day. I felt so good I didn't need my field jacket in the middle of the winter.

The Infirmary, that I was destined to visit so many times during the Fall and Winter of 1969 and 1970, was a single story building that stood high off the ground. There was a line of almost soldiers every morning waiting on the medics to have their coffee and donuts.

Once, the guy in front of me was complaining about hemorrhoids. They told him to drop his pants and lay down on the gurney and they promptly lanced them. Note: Do not complain about hemorrhoids.

My most exciting visit was when we all had to have our shots for overseas duty. As we were standing in yet another line the medics were on each side of us with air guns warning us not to move or they would cut us like a knife.

Sure enough one guy moved and it cut him like a knife. Blood was a plenty; I am sure he took some stitches.

The medics told everyone to run out the door instead of walking to keep them from passing out. That seemed like a good idea. Problem was the Infirmary was as I said, rather a high set building. It had between eight to ten steps as I remember.

We began betting if a soldier would make it down them before he passed out, just by looking at them when they came out the door. Several did not make it. It was very entertaining and additional work for the medics.

The good news was we didn't have to get a haircut while we waited to see what the Army's final decision would be. The bad news was constant KP in the day and Fire Watch at night.

This Baker's Dirty Dozen was a "Purdy bunch." The medical conditions ranged from terminal acne, dislocated shoulder, crutches for legs, ankles, feet to multiple scars and abrasions.

There were only four of us that you could not easily tell what their medical problem was.

These are the guys that I shared the rest of my Army career, talking about our hometowns and our families.

Jim was from Chicago; he was the oldest at 25 and had terrible feet. He was flat footed with gnarly toes that did not want to fit in his boots. Marching for miles would almost cripple him; he felt his family business needed him more than the Army.

Steve from Louisiana had a very bad motorcycle wreck. The screws and plates in his leg were coming apart and he carried his x-rays to prove it.

Sam was from Chicago; a big black guy who had "run numbers" back home. He was always offering to loan money at high rates of interest, but everyone liked him. He never told us what his medical problem was; barracks rumors usually revolved around a possible drug addiction.

Nick from New York had a permanently dislocated wrist. He liked to show pictures of his wife in next to nothing. The rule was, you had better look and tell him how good she looked.

Sheppard from Wisconsin had acne all over his body that was so bad that he was in constant pain. He did much better in the cold weather up north than in the humid south.

Ryan was from California and he had the ability to dislocate his shoulder at a moment's notice. It was impressive!

Then there was William. He was a "self-cutter"; lots of scars—never said much.

Robert was from Ohio. He could not hear thunder, too much loud heavy metal music. Shane had bad knees. Tim was a red head that couldn't go outside without getting sun burned.

Anthony from Louisiana had been a quarterback for LSU; one too many concussions for him. He could run up a flight of stairs and his nose would bleed. Nice, Nice guy.

Jackson had a bad back. If he was faking it, he did a great job.

At that time in the Vietnam War or conflict, as the government called it, each day the news broadcast the body count for the day. We believed that they were under reporting.

Dead was dead! Like most men being drafted these men did not want to go.

Many late nights in the barracks, before a doctor's appointments, you could hear screaming from the latrine. Shane would have some of the guys beat his knees with the end of his crutches to make his knees swell.

Sheppard wore the same bloody t-shirt that he never washed from terminal acne. Ryan would dislocate his shoulder. William just kept cutting himself. Most of the guys, including me, never had to do anything but show up for our appointments.

Within a few months we had all been discharged. We went back to our homes and families and the rest of our lives. By the way, after I got a medical discharge I was told the average life expectancy of a helicopter pilot was 30 min.

Over the years I wondered what happened to some of these guys. I am sure some died young anyway. I often watched the evening news and wondered "what if..."

*****

A "Sarge" Memory

By former USAFR SSgt James Barton
Honorably Discharged

The most important "Sarge" memory—and by far the most enduring—actually happened to someone else. I was walking through a hangar with another Airman and heard a commotion. Concerned that someone was hurt, my friend and I turned the corner and ran over to the source—a short, stocky Master Sergeant that looked like he could take out a platoon of the enemy all by himself.

He was beside himself in anger—not the manufactured anger of a drill instructor, but rather the tone one hears when a parent yells at a child who just ran into the street and is almost killed by a passing car.

The airman—young, very strong, and towering over the Master Sergeant—was so frightened I thought he might collapse. The Master Sergeant's words will ring in my head until the day I die: "You forgot?! You For-GOT?! YOU'RE a bomb loader: YOU. CAN'T. FOR-GET!!!" It wasn't clear what he forgot—my friend and I high tailed it out of there before something went off , and the lack of a mishap indicates that perhaps it was only a minor infraction.

But the message was clear and irrefutable—this isn't a grocery store we work in: When we make a mistake, someone can die. Bomb loader or not, that is the commonality with the military: One small error can mean the difference between life and death.

*****

Some of My Favorite Quotes

By Larry Payne, CMSgt, USAFR (Ret)

Some of my favorite quotes were from *Full Metal Jacket*, I promise to try not to plagiarize Gunny.

When I first got into the Air Force I knew smart ass answers were the norm. I was selected as a squad leader in basic because of height not leadership ability. The drill instructor a Tech Sergeant Armstrong pinned the badge of honor on me and I said "I will do my best sir."

He said "I know you will but you will screw up and I will take it back so don't get used to it." At the end of basic I still had the badge and told him with pride that I got to keep it. He stated, "There you go screwing up, mule face, you didn't think you could take it with you did you, dumb ass."

I was always the one to pray prior to each mission especially in Vietnam. I had a young second gunner by the name of Dino; he told me during a mission that I had failed to pray prior to the flight saying that it gave him great comfort to see me praying. I told him he needed to remember a few things about me. "The first thing I'm just the messenger, not the receiver."

"Two, I only pray for those that may die by my hands today. Three if I should die today that my family knows that I am with the receiver. Four that you die with me because your sorry ass standing there with me will make me look good."

On one occasion during a very hard mission we were receiving almost as much as we were dishing out. The co-pilot was sitting in the driver's seat trying to get certified as a pilot. The pilot was sitting in the co-pilot seat and was riding the rudder. When that is done your weight and everything you carry doubles in weight.

That 119 pound ammo can becomes 238 pounds instantly. He had caused me to drop the ammo twice so I decided to tell the pilot (co-pilot) to tell the co-pilot (pilot) to get off the rudder. Gunners are in direct contact with the pilot via gunner's hot mike. The pilot said "No" so I stopped loading guns in a gun fight, climbed into the cockpit slapped the pilot in the head with a checklist and told him he was in charge and tell the f-----g co-pilot to get the f--- off the rudder or he would be shooting his pistol at the enemy. He quickly told the co-pilot to stay off the rudder.

I have been involved in every conflict since Vietnam in one fashion or another. You realize early in a military career that promotions get you out of work but into decision making.

I never tried to put off till tomorrow what needed to be done today. On one such occasion I was in Diego Garcia being the Command Chief for the Wing there. We had a Full Bird as the PACAF commander and I worked for Lt Col Mooney.

The Full Bird was having problems with his men getting drunk and terrorizing the local bus drivers so he ordered the First Sergeants to play police and ride the buses after midnight. I strongly protested this since the shirts worked for me. I told him I could correct it and I got one First Shirt (Kelly) to go with me that night. We got on the bus at midnight at the enlisted club where all the young drunks get on the bus to go to a British owned club.

As they were entering the bus, one of the last drunks grabs the overhead rails and hangs upside down. We are in uniform, Kelly, a Master Sergeant tells him to get down. The young airman tells him to f--- off.

I then stood up and slapped the airman across the left side of his face and he fell to the floor. I then reached over Kelly pulled him up and slapped him on the right side of the face. Then in a loud voice I told him and the bus that if I had to get on the bus again at midnight to get war fighters to act like grown men then the next time I will pull ID cards and take stripes. No First Shirt ever rode the bus again after midnight.

I didn't only have trouble from young airman but also senior enlisted. One in particular was a Master Sergeant who had just got activated for 9-11 as was his wife a nurse.

I was required to get dependent information so that if both went off to war someone was there to take care of the children. I had asked him to fill out the proper form but he refused by stating that it wasn't legal and that he might as well give me the keys to his gun safe.

I then gave him a direct order and sent him to the JAG's office to get it from them. After his visit with the JAG he decided that he would skip me and go to work. I waited until noon for his return and then sent for his supervisor and him. When he arrived I had the commander in my office. The first thing I discussed was the need for someone the children recognized to take care of them not a designated day care.

I didn't give a damn about what he has in his gun safe unless it was one of the kids. I then told him that if he ever disobeyed a lawful direct order again he would be prepping bombs as an airman and it gave me great concern as to his ability to lead. Just a post note he turned out to be a good leader and is now Chief over the bomb dump (go figure!).

In Thailand I was removed from being a gunner and made a scanner. Basically what a scanner did was hang out the back of the gunship at 10,000 feet with nothing between him and mother earth but a cargo strap attached to his parachute harness.

This gunship was equipped with 4 mini's and 2 each 20MM Gatling guns. Mini's fired 6000 rounds per minute and the 20's fired 4200 RPM.

Our mission was to fly night missions over the Ho Chi Min trail over Laos and North Vietnam. We searched out weapon transports and killed them. Once you fired the 20's you were a target for Anti-Aircraft-Artillery, (AAA).

They nicknamed me Spider Man, one I was 6ft 4in tall and weighed 165 pounds, two I had a sixth sense when it came to calling the direction of AAA. Not only could I call it but count it and identify it.

They even painted a Spider-man on the back of my helmet. The basic calls when avoiding AAA were "break left" or "right" and "stall." There is no reverse.

The left scanner (me) looked straight down at the ground and the right scanner looked mainly at the horizon. The right scanner saw everything after it passed me. The good ones just shut up and relied on the left scanner to call everything.

One Christmas night we were on target killing tanks on the trail and the Vietcong were firing red, green, blue and white tracers at us.

It had put us all in the Christmas spirit. We had a gun fighter F4 Phantom with napalm and 500 pounders helping us deliver presents to the Vietcong. I was calling his strikes by giving him the clock position of the AAA being fired at us.

That is when I saw something I had never seen before, in the middle the jungle during the AAA barrage I saw the signature figure 8 flash of a SAM missile (SAM stands for surface to air missile).

I was screaming "SAM, SAM break right!" and the right scanner was calling "break left." The engineer was feathering the engines and the pilot wanted to know who the hell SAM was and flew a straight line.

The F4 knew, because we were in direct contact with one another. He hit his afterburner causing the SAM to divert to him while I watched a white telephone pole go past the back of our ship close enough to read the serial number and Russian insignia.

The right scanner and I had a come to Jesus meeting after the mission after we cleaned our britches out. P.S. The SAM chased the F4 lost contact and detonated above and behind us. I got to meet the Pilot of the F4 and thanked him for saving our lives and got a ride in his plane. But that is a story for another page.

*****

The Best Soldier I Ever Met...

By former US Army Captain Marvin Sprouse
Honorably Discharged

I am alive today because my platoon sergeant in Viet Nam pulled me out of a few bad train wrecks. Here is an article I wrote about him. Thanks for reading.

In 1965 I was the Recon Platoon Leader in the 2/5th Battalion of the 1st Cav Division. If there is anything worth mentioning in my life it is the fact that I led troops in Viet Nam, in combat situations, and was fortunate enough to bring all the men who served with me home alive.

I owe that fact to the magnificent Grace of God and to the extraordinary presence and hard work of my Platoon Sergeant, Rogelio "Roy" Salinas.

Not only was Sergeant Salinas one of the most courageous men I ever knew, he was, hands down, the funniest man I ever knew. He was constantly coming up with some gag or comment that kept me and the men in my platoon laughing our way through some world-class-terrible situations in Viet Nam.

You might have seen the movie portrayal of the Battle at LZ X-Ray, titled *WE WERE SOLDIERS*. My platoon was the first unit to arrive to reinforce Lieutenant Colonel Moore's Battalion at X-Ray. Colonel Moore assigned us the mission of recovering bodies of his soldiers, which were lying in front of the perimeter.

Sergeant Salinas and I approached a Sergeant on the perimeter to effect a crossing of the lines, just as we had been taught back at what we called "The Fort Benning School for Boys." We were supposed to exchange information about the defensive perimeter and the enemy activity to our front. That did not happen.

What did happen was that we found a Sergeant lying in the dirt, staring off into space, in a look we all came to call the "1000 meter stare." His "Briefing" consisted of his repeating, in a gravelly voice, "They're out there."

For the rest of our tour in Viet Nam I could count on Sergeant Salinas walking behind me during times when things looked really scary, and whispering in my ear, in his imitation of the Sergeant back at X-Ray, "They're out there."

Sergeant Salinas was about 10 years older than most of the troops we led. Often soldiers would ask him how he managed to walk, run and keep going hard and fast, when we were all dragging our hineys. In response Sergeant Salinas would point to the Ranger Tab on his shoulder and ask, "Can't you read?"

Only a few months ago, after almost 50 years of wondering where Sergeant Salinas was on Planet Earth, I found that he was living in Tennessee. When we finally reconnected he told me that he had been an instructor at the Army Ranger School for nine years, and had retired as a Command Sergeant Major, a top soldier of the enlisted ranks.

Sergeant Salinas told me that his wife of 34 years had died over ten years ago, and that he was engaged to marry again in a month. I promised the bride of Roy Salinas a lot of laughter. When Sergeant Salinas told me about the loss of his wife I asked him about a story I had heard.

I asked, "Sergeant, I heard, back at Fort Benning, that you had five wives, and were wanted for bigamy." In true form Roy laughed hard and told me, "I started those rumors just to have some fun."

Life is hard, and sometimes we think we can't make it. Please take and use the wisdom I learned from Roy Salinas. Laugh at adversity. Life is hard, and sometimes we think we can't make it. Please take and use the wisdom I learned from Roy Salinas, laugh at adversity and keep going.

*****

Serving in the US Marine Corps can be Demanding

By Michael R. Knapp, MSgt, USMC (Ret)

Serving in the United States Marine Corps can be a demanding and challenging occupation. With all the demands on your plate it can be frustrating as well. Many times enlisted personnel butt heads with officers. Sometimes the enlisted personnel failed to live up to standards and sometimes officer leadership failed.

I served with many fine officers and enlisted alike.

There were several officers that stood out to me in good and bad ways. Thankfully most officers were wonderful leaders.

While serving aboard an aircraft carrier I was the Aviation Ordnance Chief for a Marine F-18 Squadron. We flew many missions into hostile areas such Bosnia and Iraq. The workload on the maintenance crews and pilots was massive to say the least.

The duties of the ordnance division is to maintain the weapons systems, load, unload and arm and de-arm the weapons (bombs, missiles, rockets and guns) of the aircraft. It is a grand mixture of heavy grunt work and electronic testing and troubleshooting. Without the weapons on the aircraft, the flight is just another one man airline flight.

The ordnance division takes the work very seriously. The safety of the personnel on the ship, the pilots and the ground troops depended on it.

*****

Don't Miss "Major Snooty"

By Michael R. Knapp, MSgt, USMC (Ret)

"Major Snooty" was an extremely intelligent and well educated man. He worked in the squadron as not—just a pilot, but as the assistant maintenance officer. Often during maintenance meeting he would feel the need to address the maintenance personnel present. If there was a problem, he would need to give his take on it.

It would always start with "Let me put it in words you can understand." In other words "you're a bunch of uneducated enlisted fools so I will have to dumb down the message so you might be able to comprehend my superior intelligence."

Now I am no rocket scientist (oh wait, I guess I was) but I feel I have a fair grasp of the king's English and can on occasion understand what is being said to me. One time he did this and I acted very stupid and asked him if he could slow down a bit as I was having a hard time understanding.

The other 15 or so Marines in the meeting dropped their heads and tried not to laugh out loud. "Major Snooty" did not catch on that I was being sarcastic and then proceeded to dumb the message down even further.

I don't think "Major Snooty" ever understood that his attitude of superior intelligence made the enlisted personnel resent him. I vowed that I would not fall into the same trap when I spoke to the troops.

While flying combat missions in "the arena" (Bosnia), "Major Snooty" confronted me about a problem he was having with a particular air to air missile on his latest flight. A typical ordnance load during the flight would be two Sidewinder air to air missiles and one or two medium range air to air missiles.

The Major informed me that one of the Sidewinder missiles was not responding properly and he would not have been able to fire the missile if needed. I assured him that I would have the system checked and fix the problem.

"Major Snooty" was not satisfied that I understood the gravity of the situation. "Snooty" then gave me a lesson on the math involved. He said that if he only had two Sidewinder missiles on board the plane, and one was not working then he only had one to use.

Hmmm, lets us work out the complicated math formula. Two minus one equals one.

This conversation with "Major Snooty" went on for probably ten minutes. At this point my level of tolerance of being spoken to in this manner was quickly starting to dwindle. At the end of the ten minute lesson on basic math, I assured "Major Snooty" that we would resolve the problem before the next flight.

"Major Snooty" continued to question my understanding of the seriousness of the situation. At that point I decided I would leave the conversation and informed him that he should make sure that he did not miss with his remaining missiles.

I could tell that he was infuriated with my answer, but I said it and that was that. About 30 minutes later I received a visit from my Ordnance Officer, Gunner Holobinko. Gunner Holobinko was a fine officer and I have the utmost respect for him.

"Major Snooty" had obviously spoken to the Gunner about this. Gunner asked me about the conversation with "Major Snooty." I told him what the Major said and what I said. He laughed and told me to be careful in my words to "Major Snooty" and then said "don't miss, that's a classic."

As a side note, we checked out the aircraft and missile and found no discrepancies. A subsequent pilot flew the same aircraft with the same missile and reported that the system worked properly. I am certain that with "Major Snooty's" superior intelligence that in no way could the problem have been pilot error.

Major, no one likes to be spoken to like they are stupid.

*****

Sperm Whales and the Marine Corps

By Michael R. Knapp, MSgt, USMC (Ret)

I recall a time when I was a young Sergeant. I was very frustrated with many things that were going on in the Corps at that time. Drug use was rampant among enlisted and officers alike, paperwork for the most simple of tasks was unbelievable. The situation in the Corps was not "can do."

It was more like "why bother." I expressed my frustration to my Commanding Officer, Lt Col Sellers. He sat me down and asked me, "Do you know what one of the largest animals in the world is?"

At this point I am thinking the ole man has lost his mind. I express concerns for our Corps and he wants to talk about animals. He obviously saw the bewildered look on my face and said to me that "the largest animal in the world is the sperm whale."

Alright then... So now I am thinking sperm whale and Marines. We are "soldiers of the sea" so maybe there is a connection. The shipper then asked me if I knew how big the throat of a sperm whale is. I replied no. The skipper held up his hands joining his two thumbs together and his two middle fingers together forming a circle.

He said that "this is how big the throat of a sperm whale is." By now I am thinking that one of us is bucking for a mental discharge. Probably me.

The skipper then asked me if I knew why the sperm whales throat is only this big. I said no. The Skipper then said to me "that's just the way it is!"

I learned a valuable lesson that day. Sometimes things are the way they are because "that's just the way it is!"

*****

"The true soldier fights not because he hates what is in front of him, but because he loves what is behind him."

—G. K. Chesterton

Hats Off to Mrs. Lori Kimble

Several years ago Lori was a 31 year old teacher and proud military wife. She was a California native living in Alabama, here is her story:

Stand Up—Speak Up[3]

By Lori Kimble

It could have been any night of the week, as I sat in one of those loud and casual steak houses that are cropping up all over the country. You know the type—a bucket of peanuts on the table, shells littering the floor, and a bunch of perky college kids racing around with longneck beers and sizzling platters.

Taking a sip of my iced tea, I studied the crowd over the rim of my glass. I let my gaze linger on a few of the tables next to me, where several uniformed military members were enjoying their meals. Smiling sadly, I glanced across my booth to the empty seat where my husband usually sat.

Had it had only been a few weeks since we had sat at this very table talking about his upcoming deployment to the Middle East? He made me promise to come back to this restaurant once a month, sit in our booth, and treat myself to a nice dinner.

He told me that he would treasure the thought of me there eating a steak and thinking about him until he came home.

I fingered the little flag pin I wear on my jacket and wondered where at that moment he was. Was he safe and warm? Was his cold any better? Were any of my letters getting to him?

As I pondered all of these things, shrill feminine voices from the next booth broke into my thoughts. "I don't know what Bush is thinking invading Iraq. Didn't he learn anything from his father's mistakes? He is an idiot anyway; I can't believe he is even in office. You know he stole the election."

I cut into my steak and tried not to listen as they began an endless tirade of running down our president. I thought about the last night I was with my husband as he prepared to deploy. He had just returned from getting his smallpox and anthrax shots and the image of him standing in our kitchen packing his gas mask still gave me chills.

Once again their voices invaded my thoughts. "It is all about oil, you know. Our military will go in and rape and pillage and steal all the oil they can in the name of freedom. I wonder how many innocent lives our soldiers will take without a thought. It is just pure greed."

My chest tightened and I stared at my wedding ring. I could picture how handsome my husband was in his mess dress the day he slipped it on my finger. I wondered what he was wearing at that moment.

He probably had on his desert uniform, affectionately dubbed coffee stains, over the top of which he wore a heavy bulletproof vest.

"We should just leave Iraq alone. I don't think they are hiding any weapons. I think it is all a ploy to increase the president's popularity and pad the budget of our military at the expense of social security and education. We are just asking for another 9-11 and I can't say when it happens again that we didn't deserve it."

Their words brought to mind the war protesters I had watched gathering outside our base. Did no one appreciate the sacrifice of brave men and women who leave their homes and family to ensure our freedom? I glimpsed at the tables around me and saw the faces of some of those courageous men, looking sad as they listened to the ladies talk.

"Well, I for one, think it is a travesty to invade Iraq and I am certainly sick of our tax dollars going to train the professional baby killers we call a military."

Professional baby killers? As I thought about what a wonderful father my husband is and wondered how long it would be before he was able to see his children again, indignation rose up within me.

Normally reserved, pride in my husband gave me a boldness I had never known.

Tonight, one voice would cry out on behalf of the military. One shy woman would stand and let her pride in our troops be known.

I made my way to their table, placed my palms flat on the table and lowered myself to be eye level with them.

Smiling I said, "I couldn't help overhearing your conversation. I am sitting over here trying to enjoy my dinner alone. Do you know why I am alone? Because my husband, whom I love dearly, is halfway across the world defending your right to say rotten things about him."

"You have the right to your opinion, and what you think is none of my business, but what you say in my hearing is and I will not sit by and listen to you run down my country, my president, my husband, and all these other fine men and women in here who put their lives on the line to give you the freedom to complain. Freedom is expensive ladies, don't let your actions cheapen it."

I must have been louder than I meant to be, because about that time the manager came over and asked if everything was all right.

"Yes, thank you." I replied and then turned back to the ladies, "Enjoy the rest of your meal."

To my surprise, as I sat down to finish my steak, a round of applause broke out in the restaurant.

Not long after the ladies picked up their check and scurried away, the manager brought me a huge helping of apple cobbler and ice cream, compliments of the table to my left.

He told me that the ladies had tried to pay for my dinner, but someone had beaten them to it.

When I asked who, he said the couple had already left, but that the man had mentioned he was a WWII vet and wanted to take care of the wife of one of our boys.

I turned to thank the soldiers for the cobbler, but they wouldn't hear a word of it, retorting, "Thank you, you said what we wanted to say but weren't allowed."

As I drove home that night, for the first time in a while, didn't feel quite so alone. My heart was filled with the warmth of all the patrons who had stopped by my table to tell me they too were proud of my husband and that he would be in their prayers.

I knew their flags would fly a little higher the next day. Perhaps they would look for tangible ways to show their pride in our country and our troops, and maybe, just maybe, the two ladies sitting at that table next to me would pause for a minute to appreciate all the freedom this great country offers and what it costs to maintain.

As for me, I had learned that one voice can make a difference.

Maybe the next time protesters gather outside the gates of the base where I live, I will proudly stand across the street with a sign of my own. A sign that says "Thank you!"

Gentlemen

Ann Margaret and her "Gentlemen" —from a Veteran's wife: [4]

Richard, (my husband), never really talked a lot about his time in Viet Nam other than he had been shot by a sniper. However, he had a rather grainy, 8X10 black & white photo he had taken at a USO show of Ann Margaret with Bob Hope in the background that was one of his treasures.

A few years ago, Ann Margaret was doing a book signing at a local bookstore. Richard wanted to see if he could get her to sign the treasured photo so he arrived at the bookstore at 12 o'clock for the 7:30 signing.

When I got there after work, the line went all the way around the bookstore, circled the parking lot, and disappeared behind a parking garage. Before her appearance, bookstore employees announced that she would sign only her book and no memorabilia would be permitted.

Richard was disappointed, but wanted to show her the photo and let her know how much those shows meant to lonely GI's so far from home.

Ann Margaret came out looking as beautiful as ever and, as second in line, it was soon Richard's turn. He presented the book for her signature and then took out the photo. When he did, there were many shouts from the employees that she would not sign it. Richard said, "I understand. I just wanted her to see it."

She took one look at the photo, tears welled up in her eyes and she said, "This is one of my gentlemen from Viet Nam and I most certainly will sign his photo. I know what these men did for their country and I always have time for 'my gentlemen.'"

With that, she pulled Richard across the table and planted a big kiss on him. She then made quite a to do about the bravery of the young men she met over the years, how much she admired them, and how much she appreciated them.

There weren't too many dry eyes among those close enough to hear.

She then posed for pictures and acted as if he was the only one there. Later at dinner, Richard was very quiet. When I asked if he'd like to talk about it, my big strong husband broke down in tears.

"That's the first time anyone ever thanked me for my time in the Army," he said. Richard, like many others, came home to people who spit on him and shouted ugly things at him.

That night was a turning point for him. He walked a little straighter and, for the first time in years, was proud to have been a Vet. I'll never forget Ann Margaret for her graciousness and how much that small act of kindness meant to my husband. I now make it a point to say thank you to every person I come across who served in our Armed Forces. Freedom does not come cheap and I am grateful for all those who have served their country.

A Tribute to Craig Mitchell Dix

By Bob Anderson

A long time ago, a kid left Livonia, Michigan. He went to war. He was probably a lot like me I guess, although I never met him but he has been a part of my life daily since 1975.

In 1975, I was stationed at Clark AB, when the last Americans and a host of Vietnamese left Viet Nam. Clark had been the reception point for the returning POWs. One of my brother Cops had the wonderful opportunity to give his to the person named on the bracelet

Most everyone was wearing POW/MIA bracelets at Clark in '75. My guy's name was Specialist Craig M. Dix. The date was simply 3/17/71. Over the years, my body chemistry ate the bracelet. I had one made out of stainless steel.

Eventually the day-to-day wear resulted in so many scratches the name was unreadable. Over the years I've had three or four made. When I got to go to the Wall the first time, it was in 1996, I left the bracelet at the wall for Craig. There I found out he was listed KIA and he was from Livonia, Michigan.

After about six weeks, I could not take it any longer. I felt naked without the bracelet. I contacted a Veterans group and asked specifically about him.

When the new bracelet arrived, I found he had been promoted from Specialist to Staff Sergeant. I never knew Craig. I finally saw a picture of him. I have never met any of his family or friends.

Should any of you that knew him read this book, know that someone else somewhere else remembers your son, your brother, your friend, your loved one.

He is damn sure not forgotten!

Information below is provided with permission to print from
www.TaskForceOmegainc.org

Craig Mitchell Dix
Staff Sergeant
128TH AHC, 11TH AVN BN, 12TH AVN GRP, 1 AVN BDE
Army of the United States
05 December 1949 - 27 October 1978
Livonia, Michigan
Panel 04W Line 054

In the aftermath of Operation Lam Son 719 (Feb 1971), combat operations were conducted in areas of Cambodia adjacent to the South Vietnamese border. Like Lam Son, air transport and cover were provided by U.S. forces, while SVN Army forces conducted the ground operations.

On 17 March 1971, a combat assault was conducted northwest of the village of Snoul, in Kratie Province, Cambodia. During the assault, a UH-1H HUEY (hull number 69-15664) of the 128th AHC, 11th CAB, was hit while departing the landing zone and crashed just north of the LZ. The crew consisted of:

- WO1 James H. Hestand, pilot
- CW3 Richard Lee Bauman, copilot
- SSgt Craig Mitchell Dix, crew chief
- SSgt Bobby Glenn Harris, gunner

Sergeant Harris was thrown from the helicopter before impact and the other three men managed to exit the downed aircraft and attempted to evade the enemy troops.

Shortly afterwards a second helicopter, this one an AH-1G *COBRA* gunship (hull number 69-17935) from A Troop, 1st Squadron, 9th Cavalry, was struck by ground fire and crashed into the jungle less than a mile west of the Huey's crash site. The *COBRA* crew consisted of Captain David P. Schweitzer, pilot, and 1st Lt Lawrence E. Lilly, co-pilot.

SAR forces managed to extract CPT Schweitzer but were forced to depart the area before Lilly could be extracted. When friendly ground forces reached the crash site, Lilly was found to be dead but his body could not be recovered (Note: his remains have never been repatriated).

At this point, one man—Lilly—was known to be dead; Schweitzer had been picked up; and the four men from the HUEY (Hestand, Dix, Harris, and Bauman) were on the ground amidst enemy troops. These four men were not rescued. Since there was no convincing evidence of their death they were placed in MIA status.

James Hestand was captured later that day and remained a POW until release on 12 February 1973 during Operation Homecoming. During his debrief he reported that Craig Dix had been shot in the right ankle as he evaded approaching VC troops.

He added that SP4 Dix was ambulatory and still evading at the time of his own capture. Hestand stated that when he last saw CW2 Bauman, Bauman was alive, in good condition, and was with SP4 Dix. Finally, he stated that he saw the body of Bobby Harris outside the aircraft after the crash and believed that Harris was dead. Even so, Harris was maintained in MIA status until 1979.

While there were conflicting intelligence reports regarding the number of Americans captured and their status, two facts remain: Both Dix and Bauman were alive and mobile when last seen, and neither one has been seen since.

On 27 October 1978 the Secretary of the Army approved a Presumptive Finding of Death (PFOD) for now—Staff Sergeant Craig Dix. PFODs for Bauman and Harris were approved on 08 Jan and 16 April 1979 respectively.

―――――――――

About Task Force Omega

www.TaskForceOmegaInc.org
(Printed with permission)

Task Force Omega, Inc. is a non-profit, tax-exempt POW / MIA organization dedicated to the full accounting and return of all prisoners of war and those missing in action during the defense of our country.

This website contains useful information, historical documents, links to other POW/MIA and Military organizations as well as a complete database with the names, biographies, and in many cases pictures and map data with the location of the incident leading to their capture or when they were reported missing in action.

This site is constantly being updated and if you find any inaccurate or missing data, or have any comments or suggestions, please contact us so that we can make the appropriate corrections.

We hope that you find our site useful and that you will recommend it to your family members and friends.

Thank you for your help,
Patricia B. Hopper
Task Force Omega, Inc.

―――――――――

A Tribute to Akki

By Bob Anderson

The following story I know is true. I was there and I knew Military Working Dog Handler USAF SSgt Luke Plemons of the 62nd USAF Security Forces Squadron, McChord AFB, Washington.

This tribute is in loving memory of his Military Working Dog named "Akki." He served our country with undying devotion and stood his last post because that's what he was supposed to do—even though doing so cost his life.

Akki died on October 2, 2005 from smoke inhalation resulting from a fire in their quarters in Iraq. Luke lost everything including his best friend. Akki was an 8 year old German Sheppard from Norway. Luke and his partner were scheduled to return home in late November. Sadly, Luke returned home without his faithful partner.

Luke and Akki were some of my "kids" in Iraq. Akki was the only one I lost. Welcome Home Luke, I hope all is well with you. To Akki I'll simply say, "Good Boy!"

*****

"The leather leash and chain hanging from the kennel represents the everlasting, eternal bond between dog and handler.

The empty kennel where he once slept represents the life that he gave to protect us, our brothers, and our freedom.

The inverted bucket reminds us that he is no longer here for us to fulfill his needs of food and water, for which in life he asked for no more in return than our companionship and affection. Rest in peace my friend."[5]

Chapter Seventeen:
Final Thoughts from the Author

Here are some things I learned in the military:

If what I was doing worked it already would have worked—therefore, if it has not worked, it probably will not work.

CRAZY! When you do the same thing again and again and again and again and again and again and again and expect it to turn out differently. If we can accept that:

- Each of us are thinking, rational beings with abilities that have positioned ourselves with relative comfort in our lives; and
- Each of us possess the ability to view and describe differences between two quantifiable and qualifiedly masses; and
- Each of us has more or less the same opportunities; and
- Each of us will experience more or less the same failures and disappointments as we go through life; and
- Each of us know people who are no smarter, stronger or better than we are, but that appear to be far happier than we are; and
- Each of us has reached that critical point in our lives where we are ready to stop what we have been doing and try something else.

Old Wisdom

Old wisdom is usually "smart wisdom." In my book *Grandfather Speaks*, I talk about the importance of ancient wisdom, the wisdom of our grandfathers. Wisdom like, "always cut away from yourself." Do you have any concept how old that statement is and how many languages have expressed it.

Nothing is wrong with new thoughts, provided they build on old processes. Sometimes something jumps up out of nowhere and it becomes historical. When I was about 18, I learned that not everyone eats mustard on their scrambled eggs. I had always eaten mustard on mine and just assumed that everyone did. That was how you ate scrambled eggs.

When I found out that was not a universal process I investigated. I learned that the only person in my entire family, including aunts, uncles and cousins who ate mustard on his eggs was my father. He started doing it during World War II because the powdered eggs were so bad.

To my knowledge I have never eaten a scrambled egg without mustard. Isn't it amazing how little things become history?

I remember hearing a story about a woman that was a great cook, her specialty being pot roast. A reporter was interviewing her and asked to watch her preparations. She agreed and gathered all of the seasonings and particulars, all of the pots and pans and began to make supper for her family and the reporter. Naturally it was pot roast.

The reporter noticed that she cut both ends of the pot roast before putting it in the pan. He asked if that was the secret to her renowned pot roast. She admitted that no the secret was in the seasoning. Why then did she cut off both ends of the roast he asked?

"I don't know. That is just the way I have always done it." The next day she went to see her mother who lived in the same town. "Mom," she said. "Why do we cut both ends off the pot roast?"

Her mother was stunned for a moment and said, "I honestly don't know, it can't serve any purpose." They went to see Grandma to ask her.

When the old woman, now in her late eighties was told the purpose of their visit and asked why both ends of the pot roast were removed, she smiled. She said, "Follow me" and went to the kitchen. Hobbling slowly along with the grace and dignity of her age, she looked to mother and daughter about to reveal a significant culinary secret.

The old women stopped and removed a small pan from the cupboard. "So it would fit," she said. Her pan, which she had gotten from her mother, was so small that it would only accommodate a roast with both ends cut off. And for four generations, no one bothered to get a bigger pan.

Clark Air Base

In September of 2000 I had the opportunity to go back to what used to be Clark Air Base in the Philippines. The Philippine arm of the World Safety Organization had invited my wife Pam and me to do a week long Counter Terrorism program for several of their industrial, business and recreational interests.

In August I had made Command Chief and having this trip and that promotion occur almost simultaneously still had me reeling.

In 1976 Clark was where my career took a turn. One day the 3rd Law Enforcement Squadron Command, Major Tom Johnson told me to turn in my service revolver we had to go to the Base Commander's office. I spoke right up and said, "Sir, whatever it is I didn't do it!"

Going to the Base Commander's office was NEVER a good thing. To make a long story short, I had been given a new job as the Crime Stop Specialist; something I had never even heard of. Over the next year and a half I had a fantastic tour and received the Meritorious Service Medal for my efforts.

That night in September we arrived at what used to be the Bachelor's Officers Quarters; now it was the Holiday Inn Leisure Resort and Conference Center. Pam was "tuckered out" after a 23 hour trip and I told her just to relax with a hot bath, "I'll be on the front porch picking up bones." As I walked through the lobby the concierge asked me (in a slightly British accent), "Dr. Anderson, is there anything I can do for you?"

Liking the attention, I replied (also in a slightly British accent), "Yes, I'd like three fingers of Gentleman Jack and a Cuban cigar (they are legal there). I'll be on the portico."

As I sat there, hearing sounds I never thought I would hear again and smelling smells I never thought I'd smell again, I thought of a book by Richard Bach entitled *Running from Safety*.

The premise was "if you could go back in time and meet yourself at a younger age, what would you tell you?"

I pondered, "What would I tell SSgt Anderson about the next 26 years of his life, if he came walking up out of the dark?" Tears were running down my face.

Finally, I took a sip of Jack and a puff off the Cohiba and decided I wouldn't tell him a thing, he wouldn't believe it anyway.

The reality is promotion to Chief Master Sergeant took hard work, dedication and luck. No one makes it because they are that good; they make it because folks along the way helped. They see something in you that you don't recognize in yourself.

Most G.I.s have an "I love me" wall festooned with awards, medals and memories. I also have my "Gratitude Wall" acknowledging those that kicked my butt when I needed it and patted my back when I deserved it.

Balad Air Base, Iraq

Early in the morning in July 2005 a C-17 landed me at Balad Air Base, Iraq. I had five different missions I had been told I was slated for scattered from Iraq to Kuwait. I figured I would be redirected once I was in country.

I reported in to the 732nd Expeditionary Mission Support Group. The senior Chief and First Sergeant took me to my quarters. I had anticipated a GP Medium (General Purpose) Tent with a cot. I was pleased to see I had part of a mobile unit with a real bed. Putting my underwear in the dresser (couldn't believe I had one, figured I'd be living out of my duffle bag the whole tour), I decided I'd grab a little shut eye before I had to report.

Before my head hit the pillow, three explosions welcomed me to Iraq.

What surprised me most the next morning on my first duty day was the incredible morale and professionalism of the troops. Three days later I received a phone call from CentCom wanting to know where I was. I said, "Balad, that's where this phone is located."

The Senior said I was supposed to be at Camp Bucca in Kuwait watching prisoners. I said, "Senior, I left you six phone messages and five emails trying to get clarification on my orders. None did you bother to answer. I've been here for four days and we've been hit five times. I'm not leaving these kids! You have a problem and I have confidence you'll be able to figure out how to fix it."

For the next six months, I saw our "kids" all over Iraq. Time and time again throughout the 93 take offs and landings and five convoys that carried me over

6,000 miles through the AOR, I arrived at a FOB (Forward Operating Base) where young American men and women stood between the remnants of a wicked regime and those that would recreate it.

As the Security Forces Manager, I dealt with Army, Marines, Air Force and even the Navy. I was honored to meet and serve with some of America's finest. I'd tell you all of the stories, funny and sad, happy and tragic, but that is for another time—maybe another book, certainly over a glass of Jack. Suffice it to say, I had the privilege of participating in history.

Whatever you're feelings about the war; do not confuse them with the warriors. We made that mistake during Vietnam.

My career held many exciting and wonderful highlights. I was fortunate that God granted me the opportunity to end that career with a "final hoorah" with true Americans doing their duty.

My return home and subsequent retirement capped a story that began on 28 May 1969. It was a "hell of a ride"; I was blessed and cursed; damned and redeemed. At least, as Patton said, "I don't have to tell my grandkids I shoveled shit in Louisiana." If you don't know what I mean, look it up.

Retirement May 6, 2006

On May 6, 2006 I retired and thought my time and connections with the military were finally over. Today, I realize that will never happen. After World War II a book was published about my Dad's 44th Infantry, it was entitled *Mission Accomplished*.

I know now my mission will never be accomplished. There are too many stories that need to be told; some good ones and some not so good. It wasn't always fun, I didn't always make a difference, but as I said to Chris Culliton:

Sir, we don't get to pick where we serve. We don't get to pick what we get to do as we serve; we don't get to be where we want to be when we serve.

We don't get to decide if we'll live as we serve; we don't get to decide how we'll die if we serve. We don't get to pick when we leave our family as we serve, we don't get to pick what will happen to them while we serve.

We don't get to decide where Thanksgiving Dinner or Christmas Dinner will be served or where Birthday Cake will be served.

We don't get to pick who we will serve with or who we serve under.

We don't get to make all of our decisions as we serve. We don't get to protect ourselves from dumb ones as we serve or determine our lives as we serve. We don't get to decide very much.

For a GI, there are few decisions, we can decide between bad scrambled eggs and bad fried eggs. We can decide between being overworked or the mission failing. We can decide to let people further their own goals or we can stand up and protect our people while they protect our country.

We can decide to get up or face the consequences, we can decide to obey or face the consequence.

There is not a lot that is positive about serving your country. It is hard, it is lonely, it can be cold, it can be hot, it can be rainy or all three. Some do a few years, they have done their duty. Some stay a long time, they have done theirs. Some make every moment of their service ugly for themselves, some make every moment of their service ugly for others

There are others that are beacons during their service. They are often irascible. They are often mavericks. They are often pranksters. They are often politically incorrect. They are often funny. They are often above the turmoil, especially when they are in it.

But they are never petty, they are part of this club, they are the matrix of this club. They hold it together for the rest of us. They are the examples of what we all ought to do but usually do not.

We don't get to pick where or when we serve; we don't get to pick a hell of a lot. In fact, I guess there are only two things we can pick:

1. Do we serve
2. How do we serve

I chose to serve and I'd like to think I did it well. In a moment of chaos, men and women rise up to do great and wonderful things. In long moments and days of turmoil, stupidity and silliness, others most often falter. Others become petty and mean. Others lose their desire to serve.

As it says on the T-shirt, "Some gave all, ALL gave some." We gave a bunch. Maybe others can't see what we gave; maybe we can't see what we gave. That's fine, we don't need to. We gave.

There is a lot I would change about the military, every G.I. can say that. Some things I would change back to the way they were; but for right now, I will maintain proper radio discipline and simply say that for now—I'm Out!

A Note from the Author's Wife

My Dear Sarge

By Pamela Anderson

Photo submitted by Pamela Anderson

The greatest honor of my life was serving my husband, while he served our country in the US military. I saw my husband serve in many capacities throughout his carrier; however, the highlights were when he served as a First Sergeant, Chief Master Sergeant and Command Chief Master Sergeant.

The memories have a wide span. It was a time filled with challenge, joy, triumph, sadness and victory.

My husband is the most honorable man I know. He served our great country with a passion and with everything in him.

He believes you are only a leader if you have people willing to follow you. For that to happen, people must have respect and belief in that leader. That is something that is earned by the leader.

My husband didn't and doesn't believe he is above anyone. He understood that the mission could only be met if <u>everyone</u> was doing their best. Mediocrity was never an option. No position was insignificant, they were all important to the success of the mission.

He always pushed and challenged those in his care (his kids) to reach higher, strive more and visualize bigger! He wanted people to succeed. He never saw their success as a threat to him; but just the opposite—the biggest reward he could ever have. The mark of a respected and successful leader—leadership by example.

I have many examples of how he led by example, but a few that stand out are as follows:

1. The Gate: When he was serving as the Command Chief Master Sergeant of the 147the Fighter Wing, Texas Air National Guard, most saw this position as a desk job. Not my husband. Being behind the desk was the least favorite part of his job. Every UTA weekend, he would be at the gate at 0530 and would greet the troops as they entered the gate. He wanted each of them to know how important they were to the mission. He wanted each of them to know he wasn't going to ask anything of any of them that he wasn't willing to do himself.

2. His "Kids": It didn't matter if they were enlisted or an officer, young or old—everyone in his unit was his "kid." He took responsibility for each of them.

3. Departure and Arrival of troops: Anytime he was aware of troops being deployed or arriving back home, he (or we) were there if humanly possible. Not only troops in his care, but troops from other units. He saw his role as the Chief spanning to all military members (wow, what responsibility).

4. Mentoring: His "kids" were always coming to him for guidance. They saw the Chief as someone who could make the impossible happen. He would instill in them the desire to stretch themselves, not to settle and most importantly—be willing to do the "hard things."

5. Career Management: He instilled that each person was responsible for their career. Don't wait for doors to open, go open it! He has a saying, "hire yourself to manage yourself." Treat your career with the same diligence and attention that you do with your job. You're the best qualified to manage your career.

So what was my role in all of this? To serve my husband as he served our country and his "kids." To have his back. Make sure he remembered things. As much as possible keep problems off his scope so he could focus on the items at hand. Be at his side as his loving and supportive wife and partner.

It meant sacrifice, challenge and rewards; all too great to list here. Therefore, I'm excited to inform you that I'll be releasing a book in the future about my stories and other military wives who found great purpose, honor and joy in the most noble of service—serving their country by being of service to their military husband.

Biographies

Those individuals who submitted stories for this book and chose to submit biographical information and/or photos are listed below in alphabetical order by last name.

David A. Bond, Col, USAF (Ret)

Photo submitted by Dave Bond

Since the attacks on the World Trade Center and the Pentagon, Colonel Bond has been the featured speaker and a number of professional and community based meetings concerning the subject of terrorism and the level of preparation (or the lack of it) he feels is evident in this country. His expertise in dealing with Mass Casualty/Weapons of Mass Destruction scenarios has made him a recognized authority.

He has been the featured guest on numerous radio talk shows and a TV special on Y2K covering potential chemical and biological terrorism threats to the U.S. and worldwide targets. He has been invited to be a featured speaker at the "World Safety organization Worldwide Conference."

During his 28 years in the Air Force (Colonel Bond retired 1 September 1992) he commanded seven Elite Security and Anti-terrorism units around the world and in April 1986, was the functional director of the anti-terrorism forces involved in the raid on Libya.

His last assignment was March Air Force Base, California, with the responsibility of securing Strategic Air Command's nuclear forces in the United States west of the Mississippi, England and Japan.

During Desert Shield and Storm, Colonel Bond was responsible for the deployment of 2,000 security personnel to secure the B-52 Bombers participating in the raids on the Iraq Republican Guard Forces and securing the bases which launched the F-15, F-16, A-10 and KC-135 aircraft from Saudi Arabia and other coalition bases. He also served as the Commander of a Titian II ICBM Missile Crew, the largest in the U.S. arsenal.

Colonel Bond holds a Bachelor's Degree in Business Management from the University of Arkansas and has done graduate work at the Universities of Georgia and Southern California.

Since retirement Colonel Bond was Vice President of Sales, Home Life Real Estate in Riverside, CA, from 1993-1996. He was top salesman in the office in 1993, 1994, and 1995. He was the top manager in 1997.

Jerry Bullock, Col, USAF (Ret)

Photos submitted by Jerry Bullock

Jerry and Lucille Bullock

Jerry Bullock "Top Cop"

Colonel Jerry Bullock retired 31 July 1981 while serving as the Vice Commander of the Air Force Office of Security Police and Deputy Chief of Security Police. In 1986 he helped to form the Air Force Security Police Association, which he has served continually as Executive Director.

Colonel Bullock was born 2 Jun 1932 into pioneer Texas families through both his maternal and paternal ancestry. He put on the uniform for the first time when he was 14 years old in the high school Jr. ROTC program at Sunset High School in Oak Cliff, Dallas, TX. This was two years before there was an independent Air Force.

In August 1953, he received his B.A. degree at Texas A & M, Commerce, TX, and entered active duty in May 1854. His first assignment was OIC of Small Arms training at the Air Base Defense School, Parks AFB, CA. Shortly after the school moved to Lackland AFB, San Antonio, TX, he was assigned to the flying training wing at Laredo AFB, TX. This was followed by an out-of-cycle assignment to the 6314th APS, Osan, Korea. On return to CONUS he spent five years at Deep Creek AS and Fairchild AFB, WA. During this time the Weapons Depot at Deep Creek was phased out and transferred to Fairchild. For two years he cross-trained into Missile Launch Control in the Atlas ICBM weapons system. When it was phased out, he returned to the Security Police at Fairchild.

At the end of that tour he was promoted to Major and spent two and a half years in Turkey as Chief of Security and Law Enforcement for all US forces in Turkey and Greece.

His next assignment was to 7th Air Force Headquarters Directorate of Security as Resources Manager. At the end of that tour he was promoted to Lieutenant Colonel and was assigned to Headquarters USAF Directorate of Security and Law Enforcement as a branch chief in the Operations Division. Promoted to Colonel in 1974, he was assigned Chef of Security Police Headquarters 15th Air Force, and next to the same position at Tactical Air Command before his final assignment at the Headquarters as the Vice Commander.

A graduate of the Industrial College of the Armed Forces and the Air War College, he holds an M.A. degree from Webster College, Webster's Grove, Missouri. He has been awarded the Legion of Merit w/2 OLC, the Bronze Star Medal, the AF Meritorious Service Medal, the Combat Readiness Medal and the AF Commendation Medal w/2 OLC.

After retirement he was a licensed professional counselor, Director of Human Resources at Tracor Aerospace and owner of a business in San Marcos, Texas. Ordained to the Gospel ministry in 1965 he has pastored four churches for a total of 17 years. He has written two books on the history of the Security Police career field and co-authored the definitive history of the career field under an Air Force contract. His fourth book is a collection of essays on the theme of Life's Like That, originally written for the San Marcos Daily Record.

He is married to the former Lucille Young of Paris, TX. They have celebrated 59 years together and have seven children, 20 grandchildren, and six great-grandchildren.

Former USAFR Lt Col B.J. Garner, OD, BSC

Photo submitted by B.J. Garner

B.J. Garner is a former member of the USAF Reserve and the Texas Air National Guard. He ended his career as a Lieutenant Colonel and currently resides in Houston, Texas. As head of the Garner Vision Center, Dr. Garner holds degrees as a Registered Pharmacist, Doctor of Optometry and an Optometric Glaucoma Specialist. He and his wife, Laura, have two married daughters and three grand-children. He and his wife are also active members of the Sagemont Baptist Church.

Bob Gaylor, CMSgt, USAF (Ret)
5th Chief Master Sergeant of the Air Force

Photo submitted by Bob Gaylor

Chief Master Sergeant of the Air Force Robert D. Gaylor was adviser to Secretary of the Air Force John C. Stetson and Chiefs of Staff of the Air Force General David C. Jones and General Lew Allen Jr. on matters concerning welfare, effective utilization and progress of the enlisted members of the Air Force. He was the fifth Chief Master Sergeant (1977-1979) appointed to this ultimate noncommissioned officer position.

Immediately following retirement from the United States Air Force, Bob Gaylor accepted employment with United Services Automobile Association (USAA), a firm of 16,000 employees with headquarters in San Antonio, Texas. Hired as a management development specialist, he instructed and promoted leadership styles that encouraged and permitted employee involvement in all facets of management.

Gaylor is now a nationally recognized public speaker, motivator, and champion of employee commitment and customer service. He was a resource speaker for The Executive Committee (TEC), an international association of CEO's; he has spoken on cruise ships and continues to address military, professional, civic and educational audiences. He averages 30 Air Force base visits annually speaking at various Air Force events.

Bob and his wife, Selma, were married for 59 years until her passing in January, 2012. Together they had 4 children, 6 grandchildren, and 2 great grandchildren. Bob resides in San Antonio, Texas.

Paul Gregg, SMSgt, USAFR (Ret)

Paul Gregg, 64 year old 3 time retiree is a native Texan, born in Houston. He is retired from over 29 years in the U. S. Air Force (active duty and reserved combined), and retired from the Harris County Adult Probation Department in 2005.

He is also retired on Social Security. Paul keeps busy with his serious hobby of wildlife and travel photography and teaching free photography and travel classes at a local community college.

Paul is married to Carol who is the senior geoscience technician at a small oil and gas company in Houston. Paul has 3 children, and 4 grandchildren who live in Florida.

Former USAF Buck Sergeant Cary Hall

Photo submitted by Cary Hall

Cary Hall, Viet Nam K-9 Air Force Cop and nationally syndicated radio host. In 1969, Cary Hall was a sentry dog-handler at Cameron Bay in South Vietnam—

the first line of defense against Viet Cong and NVA attackers who would be paid handsomely for bringing back his dog tags and his dog's tattooed ear.

For a guy who was terrified of dogs as a kid, it's safe to say he didn't expect that he and his attack dog would one day be the focus of an article in Stars & Stripes magazine.

Thirty-five years later, after moving back to his hometown Kansas City, Cary and his wife Lori, created Benefits By Design, Inc., a business dedicated to finding affordable health insurance solutions for small businesses and individuals.

Cary is now the host of America's Healthcare Advocate Show—his Arbitron ratings continue to climb higher every quarter. One thing hasn't changed; Cary Hall knows how to accept challenges and come out on top!

As a family man, a veteran and a hard working entrepreneur, Cary's passion and vision is to keep America strong by protecting and improving our national free market system, particularly in the health insurance industry.

Former Army Warrant Officer Candidate Randall Hall

"Setting here with my wife of 36 years, our youngest daughter and our 3 month old granddaughter I think about the years after my discharge," Randall said. "At this point it has been a full life of family and business." He had always wanted his own business; a retail business following what three generations of family had done.

He chose a bicycle shop and won a government contract with the Air Force Base in his hometown to supply them with bicycles, it grew. He became a member of The Base Community Council and liaison on Washington D.C. trip activities and as such was able to be part of the V.I.P. tours of Air Force Bases. They traveled in Air Force KC 10s and 135 Tankers to different Air Force Bases as PR visits. They were allowed to go into the 8th Air Force War Room at Barksdale AFB in Shreveport, LA and the underground silos at Whiteman AFB outside of Kansas City, MO. A civic leader, he sat on the board of trustees of the first solar powered college in the US; Arkansas Northeastern.

Over the years his entrepreneurial spirit took him into food franchises, Real Estate and mobile marketing technology and systems development. "I've had a great run over the years, but the greatest blessings are my family and friends over these years," Randall said. "The familiar saying,' I wouldn't be here without them', is true. I have a wonderful wife that allowed me to follow my dreams and to be part of four children and eight grandchildren's lives."

Larry W. Payne, CMSgt, USAFR (Ret)

Chief Master Sergeant Larry W. Payne retired with 31 years 3 months 3 days. He was the 1st Sergeant for the 917th Aircraft Maintenance Squadron and advised the Commander and staff on matters of health, welfare, morale, discipline and how personnel are utilized within the organization. He previously served as First Sergeant for the 917th Maintenance Squadron (the largest Maintenance Squadron in the Air Force) and Command Chief for the 917th Wing.

He is a certified instructor through the Air Force in management techniques and holds the equivalent of a Bachelor's degree in personnel management through the Community College of the Air Force. He has also served as the Command Chief over the 917th Wing acting as the liaison for over 2000 enlisted members and Officers to the Wing Commander.

He was activated after 9-11 and served 2 years in the capacity of Command Chief and First Sergeant of active and reserve units overseas.

A Vietnam veteran, Chief Payne served 4 years active duty as a weapons specialists, aerial gunner and weapons loader. He joined the Reserve at Barksdale in 1982. Chief Payne is married to Tracy they have four children Kimberly 36, Kyle 33, Rebecca 25, Rachel 20 and 4 wonderful grandchildren.

Major Awards and Decorations

Distinguished Flying Cross, Air Medal with 7 devices, Air Force Meritorious Service Medal with three devices, Air Force Commendation Medal, Air Force Achievement with 2 devices, Air Force Good Conduct Medal, National Defense Service Medal with 2 devices, Vietnam Service Medal, Armed Forces Service Medal, Vietnam Armed Forces Honor Medal 1st Class, Republic of Vietnam Campaign Medal, Expeditionary medal Enduring Freedom & Iraq Freedom,

Vietnam Honor Medal 1st Class, Load Crew of the year 1983, 1st Sergeant of the Year 2001.

Doctors Marvin and Charline Sprouse

Doctors Marvin and Charline Sprouse are authors, speakers, trainers and life coaches.

James G. Taliaferro, MSgt, USAFR (Ret)

Photo submitted by James g. Taliaferro

James Taliaferro retired from the United States Air Force Reserve on September 8, 2012. He served 12 years in the US Navy (Vietnam Vet); 23 years Air Force Reserve, Security Forces (Barksdale AFB); and was activated October 2001 through December 2002 in support of Operation Enduring Freedom, Noble Eagle and Southern Watch.

He works with the Shreveport Police Department and is assigned to Caddo Crime Stoppers: patrol, public information officer, academy instructor, citizen program unit and special events.

He is married to Janet and they have a daughter, Sarah Kate.

Major Awards and Decorations

Meritorious Service Medal (1) oak leaf cluster; Vietnam Service Medal; Republic of Vietnam Campaign Medal (2)

Major Layne R. Wroblewski

Photo submitted by Layne R. Wroblewski

Major Layne R. Wroblewski is Chief, Command Post for the 507th Air Refueling Wing, Air Force Reserve Command, Tinker Air Force Base, Oklahoma. The 507th is a 4th NAF Wing equipped with the KC-135 Stratotanker Refueler.

He was born in Oklahoma City and raised in Edmond, Oklahoma. He graduated Edmond Memorial High School and entered the Air Force Reserve in 1989. In 1994, he earned his Bachelor of Business Administration with a major in Finance at the University of Oklahoma.

He was commissioned through the Academy of Military Science at McGhee-Tyson Air National Guard Base, Knoxville, Tenn. in 1998. In his civilian occupation, he is an Ad Valorem Tax Supervisor Certified as a Public Accountant for an energy company in Oklahoma City.

Layne is married to Brooke and they have three children Sophia, Zachary and Zoey.

Major Awards and Decorations

Meritorious Service Medal, Air Force Commendation Medal with four oak leaf clusters, Air Force Achievement Medal, Air Reserve Forces Meritorious Service Medal with one oak leaf cluster, National Defense Service Medal with one bronze star, Armed Forces Expeditionary Service Medal, Global War on Terror Expeditionary Medal, Global War on Terror Service Medal, Humanitarian Service Medal, Armed Forces Reserve Medal with Hourglass and M2 device, Academy of Military Science Distinguished Graduate, Basic Military Training Honor Graduate.

Notes

Chapter 4: Being a Sergeant

1. Air Force Enlisted Force Structure, AFPAM 36-2241 Vol I.

Chapter 5: Being a First Sergeant

1. First Sergeants Academy. Public Domain Information. www.AU.AF.mil.
2. "Prayer of the First Sergeant" by SMSgt Sherry Wielgosiek. Public Domain Information.
3. *The Officer/NCO Relationshi*p, The Information Management Support Center, Pentagon, Washington DC, Sept. 1997.
4. Captain and First Sergeant Joke. Public domain information.

Chapter 6: Being a Chief

1. The Chief's Creed. Public domain information.
2. The Chief Master Sergeant Rank Chief's Induction Certificate. Public domain information.

Chapter 8: Leadership: The Good, Bad and the Ugly

1. Colin Powell. *My American Journey*, Random House Ballantine Publishing Group.
2. NASA / Navajo joke. Public domain information.
3. Major John G. Stepanek. *Army Digest*, Aug 1967, pp. 5-6.
4. Major General Friedrich Baron Von Steuben. *Regulations for the Order and Discipline of the Troops of the United States*, 1779.
5. Former Sergeant Major of the Army Connelly. The Officer/NCO Relationship, The Information Management Support Center, Pentagon, Washington DC, Sept. 1997.

6. Former Sergeant Major of the Army Connelly. The Officer/NCO Relationship, The Information Management Support Center, Pentagon, Washington DC, Sept. 1997.

Chapter 9: Following Instructions

1. Gazelle story. Unknown author. Public domain information.
2. General John Sedgwick. *Battles and Leaders of the Civil War,* Clarence C. Buel and Robert U. Underwood, editors. Reprint, Secaucus, New Jersey: Castle, 1990.

Chapter 12: Good Order and Discipline

1. Chinese General. Public domain information.

Chapter 14: Military Honors and Ceremonies

1. Missing Man Table & Honors Ceremony. Public domain information.
2. History of the Challenge Coin. Public domain information.
3. "Coin Check" Rules. Public domain information.

Chapter 16: Military Humor

1. Attaboy Certificate: Public domain information.
2. Quote. Found written on the wall in 1970, Entry Control Gate 4, Elmendorf AFB, AK.
3. Quote: Konstantin Josef Jireček, Dec 13, 1881-(July 24, 1854, in Vienna January 10, 1918, in Vienna). He was a Czech historian, diplomat and slavist.
4. How the Military Has Changed Over the Years. Public domain information.
5. The NCO. Public domain information.
6. What NCO's have noticed about officers. Public domain information.
7. 16 Biggest Soldier Lies. Public domain information.

Chapter 19: War Stories

1. Citizen Soldier. Public domain information.
2. Coming home. Public domain information.
3. Stand up – Speak Up. Public domain information.
4. Ann Margaret and her "Gentlemen." Public domain information.
5. K-9 quote. Public domain information.

About the Author

Bob Anderson, PhD. CMSgt, USAFR (Ret)
Professional Speaker, Author and Trainer

Bob retired as a Chief Master Sergeant from the United States Air Force Reserve (USAFR) with over 32 years of service.

Before retiring, he was deployed to Iraq for Operation Iraqi Freedom. There he served as the Security Force Manager of the 732d Expeditionary Security Forces Squadron, responsible for a 221 person squadron located throughout Iraq, which included two law enforcement detachments and 24 Military Working Dog Teams. He traveled just over 6,000 miles in country to address and resolve issues from the Command Level to individual troop concerns.

Previously, Bob served as the Command Chief Master Sergeant of the 147th Fighting Wing at Ellington Field, Texas Air National Guard. He also served as Security Force Manager and as the First Sergeant for the Reserve Security Force and Medical Squadron at Barksdale Air Force Base.

His awards and citations include the Bronze Star, Meritorious Service Medal/ 3 devices, Air Force Commendation/1 device, Air Force Achievement Medal, Global War on Terrorism Service Medal and the Iraqi Freedom Medal.

Bob Anderson is CEO and founder of Back to Basics for Success, LLC, a training organization. As a speaker, his unique and enthusiastic delivery style creates a desire in his audience to strive to a higher level; to move from mediocrity to excellence. He drives home the roles of accountability and responsibility—leaders cannot be leaders without them. This requires doing "hard and unpopular things."

Below is a list of military specific topics available by Bob Anderson:

- Hard Leadership—Can you Shoot Your Own Dog?
- The Enlisted Force Structure, Duties and Responsibilities
- Are You an E-9 or a Chief?
- Professional Military Education (PME) Requirements and Why
- Documentation and Discipline
- Retention—Keeping the Best
- Promotions—A Privilege Not a Right
- Leadership vs. Followership—A Double edged Sword
- Taking Care of Your People—It's Not an Option

To inquire about having Bob Anderson speak at your next military or civilian event; or to access his detailed biographical information, topic descriptions and video samples, visit **www.BTB4Success.com**.

WHEN YOU'RE IN THE MOOD FOR...

Intriguing Mysteries

Fantastic Science Fiction

Mind-Bending Horror

Boisterous Westerns

Dramatic Americana

Adventurous Suspense

Heart-Pounding Thrillers

Poetic Folklore

Gritty Crime Fiction

and more!

YOU'LL FIND IT ALL AT

www.speakingvolumes.us

www.ingramcontent.com/pod-product-compliance
Lightning Source LLC
Chambersburg PA
CBHW021242260626
47155CB00004BA/1273